Praise for *Star Shepherd*

"A story about friendship, family, and finding your way in the world—this book truly shines!"

—Jen Calonita, author of the Fairy Tale
Reform School series

Praise for MarcyKate Connolly

★ "[Connolly's] use of language and suspense is captivating, resulting in a gripping tale that is wholly original. Dark, yet dazzling, this first installment in a planned duology is sure to be popular. A perfect choice for fans of Kelly Barnhill's *The Girl Who Drank the Moon*."

—*Booklist*, Starred Review, on *Shadow Weaver*

★ "*Shadow Weaver* is a spooky thriller filled with danger and magic… A fresh take on magic and friendship not to be missed."

—*Shelf Awareness*, Starred Review, on *Shadow Weaver*

"Fans of *Serafina and the Black Cloak* (2015) will find much the same chills and sequel-primed mystery here."

—*Kirkus Reviews* on *Shadow Weaver*

"Vivid and invigorating."

—*School Library Journal* on *Shadow Weaver*

"Connolly's narrative is full of meaningful moral lessons—on the limits of loyalty, the importance of honesty, and the absolute necessity of trusting others... An enchanting new juvenile fantasy series."

—*Foreword Reviews* on *Shadow Weaver*

"This book contains plenty of action and intrigue to keep the reader turning pages. It is quick to read and contains enough unsolved mysteries to make the reader look forward to the next title in the series."

—*School Library Connection* on *Shadow Weaver*

"The theme of friendship is handled deftly here... A gripping finale reveals the truth about the 'cure' for magic, and readers will eagerly anticipate learning more in a promised sequel."

—*Bulletin of the Center for Children's Books* on *Shadow Weaver*

★ "Connolly again spins a magical tale; she deftly crafts moods and creates a sense of urgency that will leave readers breathless. The conclusion to the duology brings a feeling of relief, but a few puzzling questions remain, leaving the door ajar for future adventures, should Connolly choose to return to Emmeline's world."

—*Booklist*, Starred Review, on *Comet Rising*

THE STAR SHEPHERD

Also by MarcyKate Connolly

Hollow Dolls

Shadow Weaver Duology
Shadow Weaver
Comet Rising

the Star Shepherd

Dan Haring and MarcyKate Connolly

Illustrated by
Dan Haring

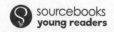

sourcebooks
young readers

Copyright © 2019 by Dan Haring and MarcyKate Connolly
Cover and interior art © 2019 Dan Haring
Cover and internal design © 2019 by Sourcebooks
Internal design by Travis Hasenour/Sourcebooks

Published by Sourcebooks Young Readers, an imprint of Sourcebooks
P.O. Box 4410, Naperville, Illinois 60567-4410
(630) 961-3900
sourcebooks.com

Library of Congress Cataloging-in-Publication Data

Names: Haring, Dan, author, illustrator. | Connolly, MarcyKate, author.
Title: The star shepherd / Dan Haring and MarcyKate Connolly ; illustrated by
    Dan Haring.
Description: Naperville, IL : Sourcebooks Young Readers, [2019] | Summary: "In
    a world where the light from the stars is the only thing that keeps the
    world safe from dark creatures, a boy, his dog, and the town baker's
    daughter must race to rescue the stars and find his father, the local Star
    Shepherd, before too many stars fall from the sky"-- Provided by publisher.
Identifiers: LCCN 2019008406 | (hardcover : alk. paper)
Subjects: | CYAC: Stars--Fiction. | Friendship--Fiction. | Giants--Fiction. |
    Magic--Fiction. | Good and evil--Fiction. | Adventure and
    adventurers--Fiction.
Classification: LCC PZ7.1.H3686 St 2019 | DDC [Fic]--dc23
LC record available at https://lccn.loc.gov/2019008406

Source of Production: LSC Communications, Harrisonburg, Virginia, USA
Date of Production: July 2019
Run Number: 5015437

Printed and bound in the United States of America.
LSC 10 9 8 7 6 5 4 3 2 1

For London, Asher, Reagan, and Presley
—Dan
For Logan, my own starboy
—MarcyKate

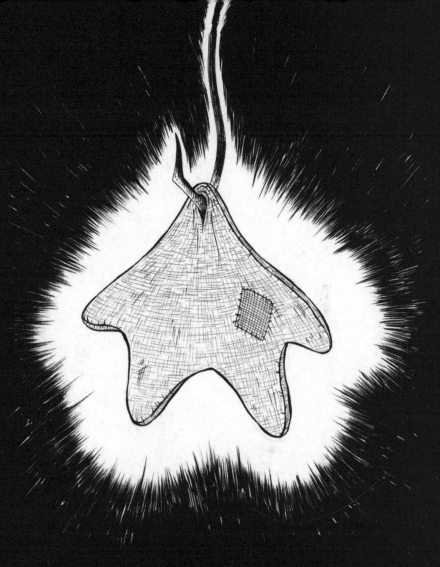

"I've loved the stars too fondly to be
fearful of the night."

—SARAH WILLIAMS, "THE OLD ASTRONOMER" (1868)

LAKE
AYSON

SELTO

THE BLACK
LANDS

COUNCIL TOWER

N

DALUTH

PEGIAN SEA

RADAMAK MOUNTAINS

RGSADA VALLEY

ROMVI

DIMOSE RIVER

RENN

KYRO'S TOWER

LAKE VOSRINTH

KELAYA

PROLOGUE

Five Years Ago

BRILLIANT LIGHT FLASHED ACROSS THE NIGHT SKY, leaving a trail of stardust in its wake. In the watchtower below, a man had been waiting for just such a sight. He and a small boy bundled up, yanking on fur-lined boots, wool gloves, and hats.

"Take my hand," Tirin said to his son, and they marched out into the snowy woods.

Stardust glimmered on the icy snowdrifts, marking their path toward the fallen star. The boy sniffled, and Tirin patted his shoulder.

"Soon you'll see, Kyro. This is how we will honor your mother. It's as if she's right here with us." Every brush of the wind on Tirin's face whispered his wife's name. But all Kyro felt was the cold.

They moved swiftly through the tall, leafless trees with spindly arms clawing toward the sky. When Kyro tripped into a snowdrift, Tirin fished him out and lifted him onto his shoulders. Above them, the stars hung brightly on their dark canvas.

"Look, they smile on us," Tirin said.

They can't replace her, Kyro thought.

The glittering trail grew brighter the farther they went, and up ahead, the top of a hill glowed like a beacon. Tirin broke into a run, then set his son down at the top. A crater lay before them, and inside it was the source of the light, the reason for their journey in the middle of the night.

Gentle warmth poured from the fallen star. Tirin dropped to his knees and whispered his wife's name—*Sanna*—like a last breath. Already the star's light had begun to fade around the edges of its old burlap casing. Tirin scooped it up.

"All it needs is a little love, and it will be good as new," he said. Without taking his eyes off the star, he began the trek back to their watchtower. Kyro trundled after him, colder than before without his father's hand to hold.

When they reached the tower, Tirin set the star on his worktable, brushing aside the cogs and bits from his clockmaker's trade. Kyro stood beside him, unable to contain his curiosity as his father sliced open the frayed burlap case and pulled out the heart of the dying star. It was a strange, molten thing, with light leaking out over its curves. His father gently set it into the new case he had worked so hard to design, one that would be sturdier and last longer. These new cases were made from glass and metal with hooks built into the design and angled just right to catch on the edges of the sky.

"When the Seven Elders first hung the stars, Kyro, they placed them in burlap because it's durable and the light could shine through. Now"—he patted his newly made glass casing—"they will shine brighter than ever."

Satisfied, Tirin picked up two tokens from the worktable—a handkerchief embroidered with the letter *S* and a small mass of gears that turned and beat in the shape of a heart—and placed them inside the casing too. Kyro frowned as he held up his own token. His father had shown him how the gears worked before his mother died, and he had managed to cobble together a token that resembled his terrier puppy, Cypher, complete with a wagging tail and cogs for ears. He set it on the other side of the star's heart, then shoved his trembling hands in his pockets.

Tirin smiled at Kyro and closed the case. Off they went back out into the snow. This time, they did not have far to go. The catapult they used to send the stars back into the sky stood at the edge of their yard. Kyro's father carefully placed the star into the sling. He let Kyro press the red button, and the gears began to whir and whine. The noise grew louder and faster until suddenly the star was flung toward the heavens. Father and son stood by watching, waiting.

The star sailed higher and higher. A little to the west of the watchtower, it stuck on the sky and twinkled as it settled into place in a silent *thank you*.

Tirin put his hands on Kyro's shoulders and led him back inside.

"Now every night when the stars hang over our heads, our family will be together again."

CHAPTER ONE

"PLEASE, FATHER, LET ME GO THIS TIME," KYRO SAID. HIS father had been a Star Shepherd for five years now, and still he had not let Kyro retrieve a fallen star on his own. But over the past few months he'd been doing his best to wear down his father's resolve.

Tirin began to object, but Kyro had already leapt up and grabbed the starglass goggles on the worktable. "It fell close by. I'll only be gone a short while, I promise," Kyro pleaded.

His father's objection died on his lips. "All right, since it's close. Take Cypher with you. And be sure not to drop the star on the way back!" But by then he was talking to thin air. Kyro and his dog were already out the door and racing through the woods.

Kyro adjusted the goggles as he ran, searching for the tell-tale heat waves from starlight that signified the location of the fallen object. The lenses were crafted by the Star Shepherd Council from stars that had fallen into the sea and went out before they could be saved. The Council oversaw the watch-towers scattered across the lands, and the Star Shepherds reported back to them every year. In return, the Council provided their home and money for food, star casings, and equipment like the goggles.

The cool night air rushed over Kyro's limbs while he and Cypher tore past the trees, dodging branches and jumping over low bushes in a burst of exhilaration. The night might have been dark and overcast, but Kyro could understand what his father saw in shepherding stars.

If only his father didn't take the whole thing so seriously. Kyro had been ready to go out on his own for months. His father didn't trust him to do it, but he'd prove he could tonight. Maybe then his father would share other things with Kyro, like the clockmaking he had shown him before his mother had died and they moved to the outskirts of Drenn. Maybe their house would feel more like a home and not just a place where Tirin slept during the day.

Cypher barked, bringing Kyro's attention to the glowing

crater nearly concealed by low brush up ahead. Excitement shivered through him. The fallen star was waiting.

He angled toward the crater and knelt down to scoop up the star. Awe filled him. His mother came from a line of Star Shepherds, and she used to tell him bedtime stories. His favorite ones were about the history of the stars. Hung from hooks fastened to the sky centuries ago by the Seven Elders, the stars eventually wore out and fell. When the world first formed, the night was filled with unspeakable horrors that thrived in the darkness. The Seven Elders made the ultimate sacrifice and gave their hearts to the sky in the form of the seven Elder Stars. They shone brightly, creating a wide net of light with beams connecting star to star, pushing the evil back into the dark corners of the world where the light could not touch them. As the people grew in number, many made the same offering, until the sky was filled with thousands of gleaming stars. But the art of giving one's heart to the sky and the secret technology of the Seven Elders died out after many years. Though all of the stars were important, the Elder Stars were the strongest. As long as they hung, the world would never succumb to darkness again.

Now a star was resting in Kyro's hands. The soft glow pulsed, and for a moment something stirred inside him. He must return it to the skies. Here on the ground, fallen stars were a long way from the Elders' magic, and when the sun rose, it would sever their connection to that magic and they'd sputter out.

With the burlap case nestled in his arms, he made his way back to the watchtower more cautiously than the journey through the woods. If he dropped such precious cargo, his father would never trust him again.

But when Cypher began to growl, his sharp terrier ears flattened back, Kyro came to a stop. The shadows were deep in this part of the woods. The trees' branches, always reaching toward the sky, seemed like they had wrapped the night itself around their trunks.

"What is it, boy?" Kyro peered at the forest. Gooseflesh broke out on his arms. The air had grown colder since he first set out. It felt like the middle of the night, but he didn't think he'd been away that long.

He ignored the fear breathing down his neck, and started home again. With every step, the chill deepened. Soon his breath was turning to frost on the air. He glanced at the clouds. The stars peeked through here and there, but they didn't seem to threaten a storm.

Uneasiness slid over his shoulders like a cold hand. His mother's words, long gone, still rang in his ears: *The stars held back horrible creatures that lived in the shadows.*

Kyro knew not everyone believed the stories of the Star Shepherds, but Kyro's mother had insisted they were real. She had been so certain that he couldn't help believing too.

"Let's go, Cypher." Kyro quickened his pace. The trees

teemed with more shadows than ever before. From the corner of his eyes, the darkness crept over his field of vision. The shadows began to take shape up ahead. Something tall and dark and, most of all, cold.

The figure moved toward Kyro, the ground frosting over as it passed. Without thinking, Kyro held up the star like a shield, the light of the molten orb inside seeping out through a jagged tear in its case. The shadow reared and backed away, leaving nothing but ice and darkness in its wake.

Kyro shivered, and his dog whined at his side. He patted Cypher on the head, his heart pounding in his chest. His mother had given names to dark creatures who would wish him harm: vissla, wraiths of shadow whose desire was to extinguish all the light in the universe; the spiderlike vritrax; scaly zintrins, and many others, all bent on darkening the world. They had haunted his dreams when he was little. Maybe when this star fell, a vissla had escaped. All the more reason to get it back in the sky quickly. "Let's hope we never see anything like that again," he said to Cypher, who still growled in the direction the shadow had gone. Kyro clutched the star more tightly to his chest.

I better not tell Father, Kyro thought. *If I do, he'll use it as an excuse to never let me retrieve a star again.*

When Kyro reached the watchtower, Tirin was pacing by the workbench. His father checked the clock and sighed. The hands edged closer to morning, but they had plenty of time to return the star to its place in the sky.

"Come, come, hurry, my boy," his father said.

Kyro set the star on the table, and his father sliced the burlap open. The new glass and steel case was ready and waiting to house the ebbing star.

Every time Kyro saw a living star, it took his breath away. This one shimmered like liquid silver but was as light as a handful of feathers. It was impossible to know exactly how old they were. According to the legends, hundreds of years at least.

His father settled the star into place and snapped the latch on the case. A silence had overcome him, as it often did lately. He cradled the star in his arms and hurried outside without a word. Not a single "Well done, son" or "Let's send it back to the sky together."

Disappointment settled over Kyro as he followed his father to the catapult. Tirin already had the star in the sling and the gears turning in preparation to launch. At first, his father had always let Kyro press the red button that sent the stars soaring into the heavens.

Now, he rarely waited for him.

His father pressed the button, and as Kyro reached his side, he heard him whisper. "It's beautiful. Just like you, Sanna."

He straightened up when he realized Kyro stood next to him. He patted his son on the head, then returned to the watchtower, watching as the star rocketed away.

When his father had first begun shepherding stars, it had filled him with purpose. But gradually it seemed to make things worse. Once, he had told Kyro that he wished the magic of the Seven Elders had survived. Then Sanna could have lived eternally, her heart given to become a star. But that magic had long faded from all living memory, and now each star was a reminder that while Tirin could save them, he hadn't been able to save his wife.

Kyro missed her too, every single day. His father never noticed that. Instead, he slept, hidden from the sun, and spent every night up in the watchtower, his gaze glued to the stars. He never bothered to make little clockwork toys anymore.

Kyro's hands balled into tight fists while he watched the star soar until it found its resting place in the sky. Cypher licked his hand and nudged his master's leg to go back inside.

Only the stars mattered to his father now. Nothing Kyro tried would change that.

CHAPTER TWO

LATE IN THE AFTERNOON THE NEXT DAY, KYRO TOOK Cypher and headed for the nearby village of Drenn with a pocket full of coins and a heart that was even heavier. He still hadn't heard one word from his father about his retrieval last night. Only "Go to the market today" and "Have you seen my goggles?"

Sometimes he'd catch his father staring off into space so absentmindedly that he couldn't possibly be paying attention to the stars. When he'd finally notice his son, he seemed surprised to find Kyro even existed.

But at least Kyro had Drenn. Life passed normally there;

people had regular jobs, like bakers and smiths and fisherman. No other Star Shepherds.

And that was how the town liked it. Kyro suspected they would have liked it even better if there were no Star Shepherds near them at all. It was hard to miss the suspicious looks and whispers when his father passed by. It was much better when Kyro came to town alone.

To the rest of the world, Star Shepherds were oddities, relics of forgotten times. Some claimed to be descendants of the Seven Elders, while others, like Kyro's father, had abandoned their old lives to become Shepherds.

And the rest of the world laughed at them.

Most people viewed fallen stars as good luck. They were made from a rare element, one that would fetch a pretty price from the right buyer. The idea of sending it sailing out of reach was mind-boggling for many, and downright infuriating for others.

Kyro had heard the rumors that his father was hoarding stars in his tower out of greed and not sending them back to the sky at all. It wasn't true, of course, but every unkind word scratched at him like thorns.

Still, when the forest broke behind him this afternoon, his heart began to lift until he felt lighter than he had in days. The gates of Drenn lay ahead, its wooden wall surrounding the village in both directions until it hit the main road in the east and brushed against the forest in the west. Sometimes he thought of Romvi, the village where he was born. Drenn reminded him of it. All those houses, all those bustling people—it was impossible to be truly alone. He missed that.

If he was lucky, his friend Andra might be working in her father's bakery this afternoon. She always made Kyro laugh. Laughter was in short supply back at the watchtower.

He walked through the village gates, Cypher padding after him with his snout in the air and tail wagging. Short houses with red-shingled roofs stretched out in row after row on either side. The main thoroughfare led to the village square and the marketplace. Beyond that were the docks and the bay that led to the ocean. Kyro could already smell the salt on the air and feel the activity vibrating through the streets as he neared the marketplace. He jangled the coins in his pocket nervously.

He really, really hoped Andra would be there today.

His first stop was the grocer, run by an old man who treated Kyro with a withering tolerance. They needed groceries to survive, and Kyro was always sure to be extra polite to the man, but it never made a difference.

Stands of many-colored vegetables and flowers lined the outside of the grocery store to tempt passersby. When Kyro entered, the grocer looked up for a moment, then sighed. Kyro's cheeks flamed. He gathered the items they'd need to last them the week and set them on the counter. The old man eyed Kyro's groceries from his chair behind the counter.

"Four silvers," he said, without getting up. Kyro handed over the coins, then took his things and left. Only Andra and sometimes the blacksmith would talk to him. Every other shop was the same story as the grocer.

Kyro stopped at the butcher, then the tailor to pick up the jacket Tirin had managed to rip on a tree branch last week. Finally, he only had one stop left: the bakery.

His hands grew slick as he approached the sweet-smelling little shop. He hoped Andra, with her dark hair and clever eyes, was waiting for him behind the counter and not her father. Bodin could be a bit…grumpy. Especially when it came to Kyro and his father.

He paused under the bright-green awning, and when he opened the door, the familiar peal of the tiny bells rang in his ears. The girl at the counter's face lit up. "Hello, Starboy!" she said.

Kyro scuffed his shoe on the floor. Andra always called him that, but it didn't sound mean coming from her lips.

"Did you finally get to rescue a star on your own?" she asked. Kyro had admitted some weeks ago that he'd been hoping his father would let him go on his own soon, and she'd asked every week since. This was the first time he could say yes.

"I did, and it's back up in the sky now where it belongs."

Kyro tried to act excited, but his father's lack of a reaction had tainted the proud moment.

"Was it as glorious as you'd hoped?" she asked.

"It sure was." He silently kicked himself. Why hadn't he thought of something better to say?

"Are you here for your usual?"

"Yes, please."

She began to put a few rolls and loaves in a bag for him, when a large, round man wearing a dirty apron stomped out from the back room of the shop. Kyro's insides squirmed. Bodin glanced back and forth between Kyro and his daughter and scowled.

"Your mother needs you out back," Bodin said, taking the half-packed bag from his daughter.

"But I was almost—"

"Now," Bodin said. With a sigh, she headed for the back of the shop, but not before sneaking a parting wink at Kyro.

He flushed red from head to toe and fumbled for the remaining coins in his pocket. "Hurry up, boy," Bodin said. Kyro managed to hand over the coins, and Bodin gave him the bag of goods.

"Now, business is business and all, but you best leave my Andra alone, you hear? She doesn't need the likes of you filling her head with silly notions about stars."

Kyro couldn't find the words to respond. His throat felt

thick, and he swallowed hard. Then he shuffled back out the door with Cypher at his side, Bodin's glare burning into his back.

Leave Andra alone? But she's the only one my age who'll talk to me. She's the only one who's kind.

Kyro's heart sank into his shoes, but as he passed out of sight of the bakery's windows, he heard "Starboy!" from the alley behind it. Andra hung out the back door, waving furiously in his direction.

He laughed. "Hey," he said.

"Sorry my father's such a grump." She walked over with her hands behind her back. "I thought you might like something to celebrate saving the star. Hold out your hand, and close your eyes."

"All right," Kyro said. Something warm and sweet-smelling wrapped in paper was pressed into his palm. When he opened his eyes, Andra had disappeared.

Maybe today wasn't so bad after all.

Kyro hummed on his way out of the marketplace, taking a bite of the chocolate cookie she had given him while Cypher ran in a figure eight between his legs. But as he took the turn toward home, something caught his eye, and he paused to squint at the sky. He snapped on his starglass goggles and even adjusted them twice, but the object remained. In fact, it was getting closer every second.

The bright, beaming thing swooped over his head and crashed into the market behind him.

Andra, Kyro thought. His cookie forgotten, Kyro raced back to the marketplace, jostling through the townspeople streaming from their shops. Smoke curled from the direction of the bakery, and when he turned the corner, he found the green awning alight with flame. A few feet beyond lay a smoldering crater.

A star had fallen. In the daytime. Kyro had never heard of that happening. Though it was nearly dusk, it still didn't make any sense.

Bodin roared from his shop with a huge bucket of water to douse the burning awning before the fire could spread any farther. The crowd murmured and gasped as they drew closer to the crater.

"A star!"

"Luck has smiled on our village!"

Bodin grumbled something about luck under his breath that made Kyro's ears redden. Cypher yapped and tugged the hem of his pants.

Cypher was right; Kyro needed to save that star. But that might mean giving up his groceries...

Before he could decide, a new voice rang out from the back of the crowd. His father's familiar form cast a long shadow over the flagstones of the market.

Tirin had arrived to collect the star.

CHAPTER THREE

MURMURS AND GROANS RANG OUT LIKE CLASHING BELLS.

"Why should Tirin keep it?"

"Star Shepherds, always hogging the luck for themselves."

Bodin stepped forward, wiping his hands with a towel. Andra's eyes were wide and worried as they darted between her father and Tirin.

"Go home, Star Shepherd. The star landed in our village. We'll keep it and any luck that comes with it." He motioned to his singed awning. "I'll need it to fund the repairs to my shop."

Kyro knew he should stand by his father, but he was afraid it would only make things worse. Bodin had no fondness for him. Cypher bounded over to the crater and growled at anyone who came near.

Tirin frowned, oblivious to the unhappy villagers. "It is my sworn duty to return all fallen stars in my domain to their rightful place in the sky. I must do so before it burns out."

Kyro edged closer to the crater. The light from the star had begun to dim. The idea of allowing it to sputter out made his skin feel tight and uncomfortable. Despite what the villagers might think, he knew the legends were true and starlight was the only thing keeping evil away. He shuddered as the shadow creature from the night before reared up in the back of his mind.

His father still argued with Bodin, but behind them, Andra urged him to snatch the star. Kyro hesitated, but when his father stepped toward the crater, a villager grabbed him by the shoulders. He tried to shrug him off, but another man joined in. Soon the crowd transformed into a mass of flailing limbs.

Cypher barked. Kyro scooped up the smoking burlap sack and clutched it to his chest, still balancing his groceries in his other arm.

"Over here!" Andra motioned for him to follow her. This time he didn't hesitate at all.

She led him into an alley, then took his arm and half ran, half dragged him along. He stumbled after her.

"Where are we going?" he asked.

Her dark eyes twinkled like the night sky. "The side gate near the woods is closest. They'll be the first to respond to the uproar."

"But my father…" Guilt stung Kyro. He should have stayed to help his father.

"Your father would want you to save the star, wouldn't he?" Andra said. Cypher yipped his agreement. "See, even your dog knows that's true."

They turned another bend and waited in the alley just to be sure the coast was clear. The guard post was abandoned.

"Thanks," he said.

"Go save that star," Andra said. "I'll try to help your father, all right?"

Kyro shifted his weight from foot to foot. Andra laughed. "Go, Starboy."

His cheeks warmed as he trotted toward the gate. When he looked back, Andra was gone.

Kyro was alone again. Cypher nudged him with his wet nose and wagged his tail. *Well, perhaps not completely alone*, Kyro thought.

They ran back through the woods. Soon the familiar spire of the watchtower rose up before him. At first glance, it seemed like telescopes dotted the roof haphazardly, but they'd been strategically placed. That was how his father knew the star had fallen and arrived so quickly in the village. But Kyro was the

one who had saved it. A small smile broke across his face. With a little help from Andra, of course.

He opened the door to the workshop and set the star on the workbench. Only then did he realize something was odd. Usually the burlap cases were torn, where age had worn the threads and the casings had torn off the hooks. But this one was different—it had a clean slice. He'd been in such a hurry that he hadn't noticed it.

Curious, he pawed through the pile of discarded casings his father kept to use as fire starters. Sure enough, not one had a clean slice.

Something like fear wormed its way through Kyro's belly.

The light in the workshop grew dimmer, and he straightened up. He didn't have time to worry about this now. The star was almost out.

Just as Kyro lifted the molten heart from the burlap casing, his father burst through the door, eyes wild. Bits of twigs and leaves stuck out of his hair, and his hands twisted as if they searched for something to grab on to. Kyro's heart slid into his feet. Hopefully Andra hadn't seen his father this way.

"Oh, thank heavens, you have the star." Tirin gulped in air. "Not a moment too soon."

His father opened a new casing, and snapped it closed the second Kyro placed the heart inside. Then he ran it outside with hardly another look at his son.

The sun was setting, and by the time Kyro reached the catapult, the star was loaded and the gears churned. Another noise caught his attention. Cypher growled at the woods.

The first villager reached the clearing as the star was flung into the heavens. Tirin leaned on the catapult. Kyro would never tell his father, but relief filled him too.

High above, the star stopped, and twinkled, and settled into place.

More villagers streamed from the tree line, frustration coloring their faces shades of angry red. The village leader, Shane, a man about his father's age with short peppered hair, stepped forward, scowling.

"You had no right." He pointed his finger at Tirin's chest. Kyro held his breath, and Cypher huddled closer to his leg.

"I'm the Star Shepherd of the region. I must fulfill my sacred duty. The stars are what keep all of us safe," Tirin said.

Kyro's heart sank into his shoes. The villagers were not pleased to hear this either. They grumbled, and shouts of "Fool!" rang out from the crowd. Kyro wanted nothing more than to hide inside, but he couldn't leave his father to their mercy.

"You *are* a fool," Shane sneered. "We never asked you to watch the stars here. We could've used some luck and a little coin. That's more helpful to us than another star in the sky. There are plenty of them to spare."

"Every star is critical," Tirin said. "Any gaps in the starlight net could have dire repercussions."

"We don't believe in old wives' tales about monsters. And our village has no place for those who advocate for them." Shane stalked back to the path. The rest of the people followed, but not before hurling a few more insults in Tirin's direction as he returned to his workshop.

Ice ran over Kyro's face as their meaning sank in. Star Shepherds weren't welcome in the village anymore. What had his father done?

And why did I have to help him?

CHAPTER FOUR

KYRO HEADED BACK TO THE WATCHTOWER, KICKING A twig on the way that Cypher ran ahead to chase. Why had he taken the star anyway? He hated the idea of seeing one die out, but if the village wouldn't help them anymore, how would they get supplies? Would he ever see Andra again? Would one lost star really make that much of a difference?

A sullen haze settled over his shoulders. When Kyro opened the door, he was surprised to see his father tearing around the workshop.

"Where did it go?" he muttered as he pawed through a pile of discarded burlap cases.

Kyro frowned. "What are you looking for?"

His father paused. "You took the star out of it; where did its case go? I must examine it."

"It's still on the workbench," Kyro said. Tirin had blown right by it in his hurry.

"Ah! Of course," he said, patting his son on the head. He inspected the case on all sides, his frown growing deeper with every breath.

"What's wrong?"

"This one is different from the others we've rescued," Tirin mused. "See!" He pointed to the slice Kyro had noticed earlier. A knot began to form in his stomach.

"It looks like it was cut, but that's impossible. No one can reach the stars. They're too high," Kyro said. Still, the longer he considered it, the colder the knot in his stomach became. Almost as cold as he'd been in the presence of that shadow creature yesterday.

His father stroked his chin. "Stars falling down in the daytime, cuts instead of tears... Something's wrong." He looked up at his son, eyes full of an emotion Kyro hadn't seen in them since his mother died: fear. "I must report this to the Council. I'll leave at first light." He set the burlap casing back on the workbench. "I will return as swiftly as I can, but it will probably take me all day and most of the night to get there, make my case, and come home. You must watch the sky in my absence, Kyro."

Kyro was too stunned that his father trusted him to watch the stars alone to object as his father's shadow retreated into the watchtower.

><☉ ☉><

When Kyro woke the next day as dusk fell, his father had been gone for hours. Nervously, he climbed the stairs to the top of the watchtower with Cypher at his heels. He settled onto the chair where his father sat night after night, one that was connected to gears and a pulley to easily slide around the room from one telescope to another.

His father had once been a clockmaker by trade, and he'd used his talents to improve the standard Star Shepherd equipment. He'd even invented a clockwork cart to make his journeys across the Black Lands to the Council tower faster. When they had lived in Romvi, his father's skills had been sought after by the rich and fashionable, but clockwork contraptions were not common in these parts. Kyro had loved the work his father made. It was special and unique.

Then his mother had died, and his father traded it all to honor her memory as a Star Shepherd.

Kyro had seen his father use this chair hundreds of times and had even sat in it sometimes when he woke before Tirin, just to see what it felt like. But this was the first time his father had ever instructed him to use it. Kyro sat up straighter, feeling taller than he had this morning. He couldn't wait to tell Andra about this.

But when Cypher climbed into his lap, and they settled in to watch, uneasiness crept in.

Could his father be right? Could something really be wrong in the sky, or was it just a fluke? With every star that came out, Kyro's apprehension deepened. But all he could see were the sky and the stars, and no answers at all.

He cranked the lever to slow, pressed the button on the arm, and the chair began its whirling pattern between the eyepieces of the many telescopes dotting the roof. Soon Cypher grumbled in his sleep, flicking his perked ears and kicking Kyro in the stomach as he chased some imaginary squirrel through the woods. The night was quiet and still. Kyro alternated between spinning in his father's chair and standing up and walking between the telescopes to keep himself alert.

What if another star fell and he missed it?

Cold desperation settled into Kyro's bones, but it kept him moving. After a few hours of watching, he finally stopped circling and went to the kitchen to make a sandwich. Cypher tagged along, no doubt hoping for scraps.

"Don't worry," Kyro said, scratching his dog behind the ears. "We'll get you something to eat too."

When he pulled out a roll from the bread box, he remembered he now had no way to get food. The thought made his appetite wane, but he knew he needed to eat or he'd have trouble staying awake. He tossed a bit of crust to Cypher, who wolfed it down and yapped for more.

Kyro threw together the rest of his meal, then hurried back up the stairs. Ever since that star fell in the marketplace, an odd sense of urgency had taken root in him. A bone-deep certainty that something was not as it should be. Try as he might, he couldn't shake it.

And he wasn't so sure he should.

Kyro settled into the chair, while Cypher, tired of moving in circles, curled up on his blanket in the corner of the room. Kyro set the chair in motion and ate. His father had crafted the chair to stop for five seconds per telescope, giving him just long enough to cover every part of the sky above their watchtower.

Not long before dawn, Kyro glimpsed something. Far in the distance, a cluster of stars was falling all at once.

Kyro leapt off the chair. He had never heard of more than one star falling at a time. It wasn't supposed to happen.

He had to do something.

Kyro turned to run down the stairs, only to halt in his tracks.

His father stood before him in his rumpled clothes, a grave expression on his face.

CHAPTER FIVE

EVER SINCE HE'D HEARD THE STORY OF THE SEVEN ELDER Stars, Kyro had liked to think of each constellation as a family. When one fell, it was the Star Shepherd's job to bring that family member home. If one died, they were separated forever.

But a cluster was like an entire family falling from the sky.

All those stars, so far away...

"Did you see it too? We must save them!" Kyro said to his father.

"We can't." Tirin shook his head. "They're outside our territory." His father hadn't been gone long, but it seemed as though the lines on his face had grown deeper and more shadowed.

Kyro hadn't ever seen his father this… Well, he wasn't sure what to call it, but he was sure it wasn't good.

"But what if no one else saw them?" Kyro glanced at the clock nearby. "We still have an hour before sunrise. We could make it there and back. I know it."

"We can't, Kyro. We must remain here and watch our own piece of the sky."

Kyro dropped back into the chair. "You're sure another Star Shepherd will retrieve them?"

Tirin put a hand on his son's shoulder. "I'm afraid not. They landed in the Radamak Mountains."

The Radamak Mountains were forbidden to Star Shepherds. The legends said that when the stars were first hung, some of the dark creatures hid there. The mountains were said to be so enmeshed in shadows that even the stars' light couldn't penetrate the darkness there.

Kyro's mouth fell open. "You mean *no one* will rescue them? We have to let them burn out?" Until recently, he had never given serious consideration to how he felt about letting the stars die. Now, the thought of letting a star sputter out on their watch filled him with dread.

Tirin sank into a nearby chair. "Some things cannot be saved."

"But it's a betrayal of the Star Shepherd oath. How can they allow rumors to keep them from carrying out their duty?"

"To many, the local villagers, for example, our care for the stars is based solely on rumors and superstition. Those dark creatures were once as real as you and me."

"But the stars hold them back. That's what you always told me." Kyro frowned and rubbed Cypher's belly. The dog thumped his tail and yawned.

"They're supposed to." Tirin sighed.

An uncomfortable silence threatened to settle over them, but Kyro broke it. "Well, what did the Council say?"

"Nothing of importance." Tirin stared at his hands and shook his head. Understanding sunk in, and with it, the sharp point of needling worry. The Star Shepherd Council wasn't going to look into the oddities of the fallen star Tirin had reported. What Kyro couldn't understand was why.

Tirin took a deep breath, as if he was weighing his words. "I did learn one thing from the Council meeting. A couple of other Shepherds have reported similar things, like stars falling in groups or unexplainable shadows bringing on a sudden cold. I believe that those shadows are the vissla, that those terrible creatures have somehow returned. There is much that we don't know. I fear the world is growing more dangerous than ever."

Kyro glanced through the telescope once more. In the distance a light shone between the mountains, and he watched it ebb. Hollowness expanded inside his chest, and he looked away.

He hadn't told his father about the dark creature he had encountered the other night. He was beginning to think he should.

"I'm sorry," his father said. "There is so much I wish I could have saved." Tirin raised his watery eyes to meet his son's. The grief in them froze Kyro to his chair.

All this talk of not being able to save the stars was bringing back memories of his mother. She'd sickened very quickly, and Tirin had not been able to help her. Before they knew it, her light had sputtered out just like that cluster of stars. That was why Tirin had taken up Star Shepherding in the first place. Kyro's grandparents on his mother's side had been Star Shepherds too, and it was Tirin's way of keeping some little piece of Sanna's memory alive.

What if one of those stars that fell in the mountains was the one he and his father had rescued first? The one that bore a little token of each member of his small family, meant to keep that memory bright?

He needed to change the subject before his thoughts became unbearable.

"Father, there's something I should tell you."

Tirin frowned. "What is it?"

Kyro picked Cypher up and put him on his lap, almost like a shield. "The other night, I...I think I may have seen one of those shadows some of the other Star Shepherds have reported."

Tirin sat bolt upright. "What happened? Tell me, what did you see?"

Kyro's eyes burrowed into Cypher's fur. "It was the night you sent me out to rescue a star on my own. I was headed back when I saw the shadows break out from the trees as one tall form. The air grew very cold, and then I just ran."

Tirin gripped the arms of the chair. "Have you seen a creature like that ever before or since?"

"No, I swear it."

His father relaxed a little. "Good. If you ever see one again, always be sure you get to the star first. We cannot let them fall into vissla hands."

Kyro frowned. "Can they even touch the stars? When I held up the star, the light seemed to force it back."

"The stars contain power that must be wielded. When they hang in the sky, the Elders' Magic wields them against the dark creatures. But on the ground anyone could claim them. Perhaps that is why someone is cutting them down..." Tirin rubbed his chin.

Kyro glanced at one of the telescopes again, and he stood up out of his chair. "Look!"

Tirin bent near the telescope too, and his face went pale.

Another cluster of stars was falling—and it was within their territory.

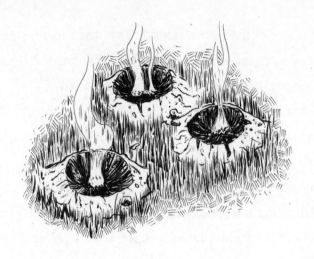

CHAPTER SIX

THIS TIME, TIRIN DIDN'T OBJECT TO CHASING THE FALL-
ing stars. They raced from the watchtower and tore through
the woods in the direction the cluster fell. The trail of light hit
the ground, and the earth quivered beneath their feet, but it
didn't slow them. Wind whipped through the trees and clawed
through their jackets, but neither of them missed a step.

Tirin banked to the left, but Kyro was right behind. Cypher
barked at them, trying to keep up. Finally they reached the spot
where the stars had fallen. The area was pockmarked by craters, but something wasn't right.

Kyro adjusted his goggles to be sure he was seeing correctly.

Not one of the craters glowed. Tirin leapt into the nearest one, and Kyro ran to the next. He fell to his knees at the edge, barely hearing the shocked gasp from his father.

The crater was empty.

He rushed to the next, only to find it empty too. And the next and the next.

Kyro turned in a circle, gaping and confused.

All of the stars had vanished. Not even a trace of their burlap casings remained. Only empty, smoking holes.

Tirin stood over his crater, tearing at his hair. He ripped his goggles off his face and began to pace and mutter.

"Who could have done this? Why? It just doesn't make any sense," he mumbled.

"Father, I—" Kyro began.

Tirin's head shot up. "You must go home. Right away. It's too dangerous out here. Take Cypher with you." He snapped his goggles back into place. "I'm going to find those stars." Without waiting to see if Kyro obeyed, his father set off into the woods.

"Come on, boy," Kyro called to Cypher, and then he headed back down the trail toward the watchtower.

Kyro was so absorbed in his thoughts that he didn't look up until he realized Cypher was tugging at the hem of his pants. "What is it?"

Cypher yipped. Kyro followed the dog's eyes and saw, to his shock, yet another star falling in the sky overhead.

And it was close.

So many falling stars all in the same night? Things had gotten very strange indeed.

Kyro found the telltale glow, and then set off in the direction of the star, Cypher at his heels. A sense of urgency spurred him on. Tonight alone, they had failed—twice—to save nearly ten stars between those two clusters.

This was one last chance to save *something* this evening.

Kyro and Cypher approached the glowing crater in the woods, but stopped short when a terrible scream, like ice crackling, echoed through the trees. He could feel the ground beneath his feet growing cold through the soles of his shoes.

A dark shadow rose up between the crater and Kyro, sending Cypher skittering behind his legs. Within seconds, Kyro could see frost on his breath. The star rested too close to the dark, giant form, and he was too terrified to do anything but watch the frost slide over the burlap sack. Kyro told his feet to run, but it was as if they were frozen in place. The shadow creature molded part of its darkness into a long scythe and sliced the star open.

"Stop!" Kyro said, but the shadow paid him no attention. Where was his father? Surely he could banish this creature.

The dark figure reached into the fallen star and yanked out the heart. The light extinguished in its palm as the star froze over. Then the shadow creature squeezed its dark fingers closed, and the star crumbled into ice and dust on the forest floor.

"No!" Kyro cried, his limbs finally lunging toward the stardust, but it was too late. The dark shadow was already melting into the trees, and the star was long gone. And with it, all the hope that had filled Kyro moments earlier.

He sank onto the cold earth, head in his trembling hands. He couldn't deny what that frightening shadow creature was. It looked just as his mother had described the fearsome, cold vissla.

When the stars were first hung and the starlight net formed by interconnected beams of light, the dark creatures were banished underground and to the darkest corners of the world. It was rumored that some even hid in the Radamak Mountains and beneath the ashy sands of the Black Lands. But the sunlight and starlight held them prisoner in those places, unable to roam freely across the world as they had long ago.

But now that there were gaps, holes in the starlight net, were the dark creatures beginning to break free of their dark prisons? Could they wander in the darkness where there was once light? The sun protected the world during the day, and the stars were supposed to protect them at night. They had for centuries. Kyro shivered and hugged his knees. Cypher licked his face.

Kyro shook off the circling vultures of thought and got back to his feet. There was nothing he could do for any of the stars that had fallen tonight. "Let's go home, Cypher."

When they reached the watchtower again, Kyro was exhausted and immediately fell asleep on his cot, haunted by dreams of dying stars.

CHAPTER SEVEN

KYRO WOKE TO THE SOUND OF THE WATCHTOWER DOOR slamming shut and Cypher whining by his bedroom door. Kyro got up to let the dog out and found his father, disheveled and harried, muttering to himself and shoving items into a bag.

Tirin's eyes widened when he saw Kyro. "Someone has stolen them," he said, an unmistakable quiver in his voice. "I must find them."

Kyro rubbed his eyes. The sun was up, so it must be morning now. "The stars?" he asked.

His father nodded vigorously as he closed his bag. "It's the only explanation. Nothing else makes sense. Kyro, this is very important. I need you to stay here and tend to the stars. I'll be back in a day or two."

Equal parts of fear and excitement flooded through Kyro in a heady mix. "That long? Watching by myself?"

His father picked up two large vials of sparkling powder from the kitchen table and shoved them into Kyro's hands. "Take these. Only use them if necessary."

Kyro puzzled at the vials. "What is this?"

"Stardust, of course." His father put on his coat and slung the pack over his shoulder.

"But what—"

Tirin sighed. "I wouldn't do this if it wasn't so urgent. Everything depends upon it."

"Where are you going?" Kyro frowned.

His father's face grew serious. "I can't tell you that. You must not follow me. Stay here until I return." Tirin ruffled Kyro's hair and quickly ducked out the door before Kyro could say another word.

⤛⊙ ⊙⤜

The two days Tirin said he'd be away passed quickly. Then two more, and two more after that. Soon, an entire week had gone by without any word.

Kyro grew more and more uneasy with every day that slipped by. On the seventh day he could hardly sit still. He'd never been alone for this long before. When he woke that afternoon, he opened his bedroom door and saw that his father still had not returned.

He let Cypher outside and checked the yard. No sign of his father. The cart was still in the shed out back, just where he'd left it. Kyro had thought that was odd too. Where had his father gone that he wouldn't have needed his cart?

Kyro stumbled back inside, the rocks in his gut churning. How could his father leave him? Sure, he ignored him most of the time, but to leave him all alone to fend for himself? To watch the stars by himself for this long?

He paused by the empty kitchen table. Perhaps Tirin had stopped by the village for supplies on his way out of Drenn. Someone there might have a clue to where his father had gone. And he could use more groceries too.

Kyro couldn't sit still any longer. He grabbed his coat and bag and headed out the door as fast as his feet would take him.

Night descended as he ran to the village, and he couldn't help keeping one eye on the sky overhead. No more star clusters had fallen since his father left, just a single one here and there, but it still worried him. The spindly trees rose up beside him, casting long shadows every which way. Each noise made Kyro jump, and every degree that the temperature chilled made him wonder if one of the vissla was nearby. He shuddered. He never wanted to encounter another one again.

When he reached the village, he snuck in through the side gate that Andra had showed him the last time he was there. He wasn't sure how serious the people were about his father not being welcome anymore and how far it extended to himself. Could his father have stopped here and run into trouble? Might that explain his prolonged absence? Kyro made it to the marketplace without incident but saw no ready sign of his father. A few shopkeepers were still there, but most were closing up for the night.

Kyro was tempted to stop at the bakery and say hello to Andra, but when he walked by, all he saw through the window was Bodin sweeping the floors. He glanced up and scowled. Kyro ducked his head and moved on to the grocer.

The old man sighed when Kyro entered.

"Excuse me, sir, but I'm trying to find my father, Tirin. Have you seen him today?"

The grocer raised his eyebrows but shook his head. "Sorry, son, haven't seen him since the last time he was here raising a ruckus." He cleared his throat, and his meaning sank in. Tirin really wasn't welcome anymore.

Kyro quickly purchased a couple items he needed, but didn't feel comfortable staying any longer than necessary. Then he stopped in every store that had lights on, but all the merchants said the same thing. They hadn't seen his father recently, and they were just fine with that, thank you very much. Worry gnawed at Kyro's insides as he stopped in one last shop—the steel smithy. Tirin was Doman the smith's best customer; if anyone in Drenn would care if Kyro's father vanished, it would be him.

Kyro paused in the doorway, letting the tangy smell of the smelting fires wash over him and bring a little warmth his way. His hands were shaking, and he shoved them in his pockets.

"Doman?" he called.

"One moment!" boomed a loud voice from the back of the shop. The front was lined with all sorts of interesting items polished to a gleaming shine. Swords, knives, fishing hooks, as well as an impressive array of gears and even a few star casings in the corner.

Doman came out balancing a newly crafted blade in one hand. "Kyro. What are you doing here this late?"

"I'm looking for my father. I thought you might've seen him recently." Hope filled Kyro for a fleeting moment. Then Doman's expression shifted to a frown.

"I'm afraid not. Haven't talked to him in a couple weeks at least. Stars must be falling slowly these days." Doman smiled, though something about it felt off to Kyro. But why would he lie?

"Thanks anyway," Kyro said. He wandered out of the shop and stood in the middle of the now empty market. His father had left him and gone after whoever was stealing the stars. He must have either run into trouble or completely lost track of time, and Kyro had no means to determine which it was.

He had no clue where his father had gone, and no idea where to begin looking.

Hot tears burned behind his eyes. Tirin had officially abandoned his post—and his son. Kyro wasn't ready for this, he wasn't even sure he wanted to do it, but now his father's responsibility to save the stars had truly fallen to him.

CHAPTER EIGHT

WHEN KYRO ARRIVED HOME, HE PAUSED OUTSIDE. THE watchtower rose before him, the many telescopes dotting the roof like the antennae of some bizarre insect. Always watching, always waiting for another star to fall.

But tonight, no one waited for him except his dog.

The nearest star winked at Kyro. He knew what he had to do. He was tired of waiting for his father to return. There were vissla on the prowl in the woods, and after what he had seen, Kyro suspected they were the ones stealing the stars. Something had to be done, and he was the only one left. He never again wanted to see one die in a vissla's hands like he had a week ago.

His father might have left him just the tools he needed to keep that from happening again.

When Kyro entered his home, Cypher bounded over to greet him. "Hi there, boy." He knelt down to hug his dog. Then Kyro headed for his father's workshop where he'd stored the strange vials. His mother had once told him that stardust had protective properties, but it was rare. Perhaps this was what had become of the occasional star that fell too close to dawn to save. He hoped he could use it to get an edge over the dark creatures.

Ever since he saw the vissla pick up that star, Kyro had been puzzling over how it had done it when he had been able to ward it off with a star's light a few nights earlier. What his father had told him not long before he left was the only thing that made sense: it was all about who wielded the star's power. As part of the starlight net in the sky, a star could hold back the evil creatures. And when Kyro had picked it up, he was able to use it against the vissla. But the vissla could destroy a star if it wasn't being actively used against them. The creature had done the deed quickly, as though it couldn't stand to touch the star for too long.

Stardust wasn't quite the same as a star, but Kyro hoped that it would at least slow down any vissla that came near. They were getting bolder, and there was nothing stopping a vissla from following him all the way to his front door. At the very least, the stardust might give him a few more minutes to return a star to the sky.

Kyro marched out to the perimeter of the yard and carefully surrounded it with a thin line of stardust. He studied it curiously for a moment. It almost looked like salt, but more shimmery. Then he returned home, took a deep breath, and went up into the watchtower, taking his seat in his father's clockwork chair.

Now it was his. At least, until his father came back.

If he comes back, Kyro thought.

Cypher licked his hand. "I'm glad you've stuck around." Kyro pressed the button, and the chair began its rounds.

Minutes passed into hours, while the stars performed their nightly dance in the sky overhead. Kyro had resigned himself to an uneventful evening when he heard a knock at the door.

Father! was his first thought, and he immediately realized how foolish that was. Why would his father knock on his own door? It had to be someone else.

Curious, Kyro hurried downstairs.

He opened the door to find Andra and her sparkling dark eyes. His jaw dropped, but he couldn't help meeting her smile with his own.

"Hello, Starboy," she said. "I know it's late, but I also know you stay up all night, so I thought it would be all right if you had a visitor." She hesitated, holding up the bag she carried. "May

I come in? I heard about your father, and I know the villagers haven't been very nice to you lately. I thought you might need some groceries."

Kyro's stomach rumbled in response. He had been in such a hurry to leave the grocer earlier that he had only bought a couple necessities. His face bloomed red, but she laughed. "Sounds like I was right."

"Yes, please come in." Kyro opened the door wide. When Andra walked past him, he caught the scent of freshly baked cookies, like she was bringing a little bit of that warmth into his home too.

Andra stooped to scratch Cypher behind his ears and even pulled a biscuit from her pocket for him. He gulped it down and wagged his tail, hoping for more.

Kyro took the groceries—the bag was filled with bread and cheese, along with some fresh greens, and even a little meat from the butcher. And a small bag that could only hold one of the sweets she always snuck him.

"Thank you, Andra. This is..." Kyro had difficulty swallowing the sudden lump in his throat. "This is real nice of you. I can pay you back when my father gets his next payment from the Council—"

Andra waved him off. "Don't worry about a thing. I wanted to help."

Kyro ran a hand through his dark, unruly hair. He glanced

around the small kitchen and workshop area. They never had guests, and didn't really have anywhere to entertain people. "Do you want to sit down? Or have something to drink? Eat?"

Andra laughed. "Sure, I'd love to sit for a bit."

Warmth tingled over Kyro's arms. Andra sat and folded her hands in her lap.

"Are you going to sit too?" she asked.

"Y-yes." He joined her at the kitchen table, his leg bouncing nervously.

Andra took in her surroundings. "How do you monitor the stars from here?"

"Oh." Kyro was so surprised to have Andra here in his house that he had nearly forgotten all about his duties. "Yes, I should do that. I have to go up into the watchtower for that."

"Can I see?" Andra asked.

Kyro showed her the watchtower, Cypher dancing at their heels. When they reached the landing and the clockwork chair, Andra's eyes grew wide.

"What is *this*?" she asked.

"My dad made it." Kyro patted one of the larger gears. "He was a clockmaker before he became a Star Shepherd. He used to make all kinds of things. But he really threw his passion into this and modifying the catapult we use to return the stars to the sky."

Andra ran her fingers over the arm of the chair. "What do all these buttons do?"

"It's better if I show you." Kyro hopped into the chair and pressed the button that made the chair slowly circle the room. Andra squealed when it began to move and marveled at how it stopped just long enough at each telescope to check that sector of the sky.

"Then this one"—Kyro pressed a yellow button—"goes backward." The chair did as directed. "Do you want to try it?"

Andra grinned. "Absolutely."

Kyro stopped the chair and hopped off to let her sit. Her feet didn't touch the floor, but she still sat in the chair like she owned it.

"So, which button makes it go faster?"

Kyro laughed. "The blue one, but—" He didn't get a chance to finish his sentence. Andra pressed the blue button and the chair spun on its track, careening by the telescopes. She laughed, and after two full passes at lightning speed, she pressed the button to make it stop. Her eyes were full of wonder and starlight.

"Does your father let you do this by yourself often?" She stepped off the clockwork chair, then plopped to the floor to play with Cypher.

Kyro's face clouded over. "No, not usually. Never for a full night. Only if he's feeling sick or is late returning from a Council meeting."

"Do you have any idea where he is now?" she asked softly.

Kyro sank into the chair. It was positioned in the center

of the room. He could see through each telescope from here if he wanted, but he'd need to use the chair to get a closer look through one of the telescopes if something fell across the sky.

"No," he said. "He said he'd be back in two days, and that was a week ago."

Andra put a hand on Kyro's arm. "I'm sorry. Maybe it was beyond his control. I'm sure he'll be back soon."

Kyro blinked rapidly. "Yeah, I hope so. The thing is, I think he may have done something dangerous."

Andra raised her eyebrows. "What do you mean?"

Kyro's eyes tracked through the telescopes while he talked just to be sure he didn't miss any falling stars. "The other night something strange happened. We saw not one, but two clusters of stars fall. That *never* happens. Two stars in the same night is a lot, and more often than not, none fall."

Andra frowned. "Why do you think they all fell at once?"

"I'm not sure, but I can't help thinking that something is wrong with the stars. My father sure thought so." Kyro picked at a loose thread on his sweater, debating how much he could tell Andra without her thinking he was crazy. "One of the clusters was too far away, but the second was nearby. When we went after them, all we found were empty craters dotting the forest floor. Someone took the stars."

Andra gasped, startling Cypher out of her lap. "Someone *took* them? How? Who would do such a thing?"

"I don't know." Kyro shrugged. "That's why it's so strange. My father sent me home, and—" Kyro hesitated, then decided not to mention his encounter with the vissla just yet. "And when I got up the next day, he was preparing to leave. I think he found a clue out in the forest and now he's gone after them, and I have no idea where that might be." Kyro wrapped his arms around his stomach and sank deeper into the chair.

Cypher nudged Kyro's knee, then leaned against his leg as if to comfort his master. All Kyro felt was empty and cold.

"How do you know the stars didn't simply burn out before you could get there?" Andra asked.

"Because we would have at least found the cases. All the old stars have burlap cases, and when they fall from the sky, we replace them with new steel-and-glass ones." Kyro hopped down and pulled over a discarded burlap sack. "See? This was an old casing."

"How did the stars get all the way up there in the first place?" Andra asked. She hugged her legs to her chest and rested her chin on her knees.

Kyro knew this story so well he could recite it from memory. Even before his father had taken up Star Shepherding, Kyro's mother had told him a version of it at bedtime that he knew by heart. He hadn't realized the significance at the time, that she was giving him a little piece of herself, her past, for him to carry on.

Maybe now he could pass that on too.

CHAPTER NINE

KYRO TOLD ANDRA ALL ABOUT THE LEGEND OF THE
Seven Elders. "And that's how the stars came to rest in the sky
and Star Shepherds came to take care of them," he finished.
Andra's expression was rapt.

"The Seven Elders put them there? But how did they do it?
A catapult like you have? Or were they tall enough to reach?"
She grinned.

"No, they had a little help. The Elders built huge mechanical giants who flew up and hung the stars on hooks in the sky.
My father used to tell me that's what inspired him to become
a clockmaker. He always wanted to build something that

extraordinary one day." Kyro's smile faltered. His father hadn't confided in him like that in a long time. "But we don't use burlap and hooks anymore. We have new cases made from glass and steel that are sturdier and have built-in hooks. That way we can hang the stars back in the sky without the help of giants."

"That's incredible. And you believe it all?"

Kyro paused. Was it wise to admit that he believed in it? When his mother used to tell him the stories at bedtime, he'd wanted to believe. After watching his father retrieve stars in burlap sacks and send them back to the sky night after night for the last few years, he knew at least some of it was true. And now that he had encountered that frightening, cold shadow creature, any lingering doubts had disappeared.

"I do. The stars are just as the legends say, and someone had to put them there. And…I may have seen one of the dark creatures, a vissla, recently." He twisted his fingers together in his lap. While he liked talking with Andra like this, he didn't want to scare her away. But he also didn't want to lie to her. "It's all true. And if someone is stealing stars, then the dark things might come back. I'm worried that the vissla might be the ones taking the stars in the first place."

Andra sat up straighter. "You saw one of the shadow creatures?"

"On my first solo run. The thing radiated cold, and it wanted the star. But I got away. The night before my father left, I saw another one." Kyro shuddered. "The creature got to the star first, and I couldn't stop it. It killed the star's heart. Its deathly cold burned the life right out of the poor star. All I could do was watch. If my father had been there, he could have done something to stop it. But he wasn't, and if I'm right about the vissla, he's gone off on a fool's errand. Now I don't know where he is or if I can keep the stars safe while he's gone."

Kyro's shoulders drooped under the admission he'd been holding inside all day. He'd spent so much time being angry with his father that he didn't know if he could do this without him.

"Kyro!" Andra cried, pointing at one of the telescopes. His eyes followed and saw a star flying across on the eastern part of the sky.

He sat bolt upright. Then he grabbed his starglass goggles and snapped them into place. "Let's go save it," he said. Andra grinned so wide it was nearly blinding.

She grabbed his hand, and together they ran down the stairs and out the front door, leaving Cypher snoozing in the watchtower. Kyro only paused for a moment to get his bearings once they were outside, and then they were off after the star.

"You do this every night?" Andra said as they ran.

"You haven't seen anything yet," Kyro yelled back. The pair raced through the forest, dodging tree branches and fallen logs until the glow of the fallen star grew brighter.

They reached the glowing crater, nestled between two

thick-trunked trees. The fallen star was brilliant and beautiful, and the fact that it was still there this time filled Kyro with a sudden, unexpected emotion: hope.

But he knew they had no time to waste. He scooped up the star, and together they headed back toward the watchtower, this time at a slower pace to be sure he didn't drop the star.

"When we get to the workshop, we'll set it in its new case, then send it back to the sky. That's the best part."

Andra couldn't keep her eyes off the glowing burlap in Kyro's hands. "This is much more interesting than baking."

Kyro's laugh died in his throat. A sound like ice cracking on a pond echoed through the trees, and the night surrounding them grew several shades darker.

"Hurry!" he whispered to Andra.

"What is it?" she said.

"The vissla," Kyro said, his face pale. He clutched the star close to his chest, not wanting to risk a vissla taking this star too. "We must be quick and quiet."

Andra fell into step right behind Kyro.

The crackling sound grew louder, and the air around them dropped several degrees, but Kyro didn't stop moving. All he could think about was the sad little star the vissla had turned to dust. He wasn't going to let that happen again. Not on his watch.

Kyro peered into the forest. Many yards away, something

dark and cold was moving. His breath stuttered. He grabbed Andra's hand, still clutching the star in the other, and sprinted toward the watchtower. Hopefully, the stardust would slow the vissla. He had no idea what else to do if it didn't work.

They fled the woods and charged toward the workshop door. He glanced back to see the shadow creature leave the woods, its terrible crackling ice forming a path beneath it, then balk after a few feet. It moved to the side, but again stopped. Then the other side, with no luck. A terrible keening rose up, and the layer of ice stopped in a half circle at the edge of the yard, as if blocked by an invisible dome.

Kyro gaped as he realized the stardust wasn't just slowing the vissla; it was blocking its path forward. Sudden warmth filled him from head to toe. His father really had been trying to protect him. For now, home was safe.

He flew back into motion, flinging the door open and locking it the moment Andra stepped inside. Breathless, he rested the star on the worktable.

"What do we do now? Will it follow us? Why did it stop?" Andra asked. Her hands shook, and she tucked them into her pockets.

Kyro gasped for breath and leaned on the table. "My father gave me stardust before he left, and I put it out as a ward around the yard. I wasn't even sure it would work, but that's why it can't follow us any farther. I think we're safe." He picked up the knife that lay on the table beside the star. "Now, we have to transplant this into its new home."

"How can I help?" Andra asked.

"See that pile over there?" Kyro pointed to the stack of metal-and-glass star casings Tirin had had specially constructed by Doman, Drenn's blacksmith. "Grab two of them."

Andra did as she was told, and carefully set them on the table beside the burlap sack. Then Kyro sliced open the casing and gently lifted the orb out.

The star glowed in his cupped hands, its molten light swirling and fading every second. This one had a bluish hue, with hints of red speckled throughout.

Andra tentatively set her hand on the top of the star. "It's beautiful," she said. "What a wonderful thing you do, saving them every night."

Kyro's face flushed. "We must hurry. It's fading already." He pushed the burlap aside and gently placed the star inside its new home. It glimmered once, as if in thanks, before Kyro closed the case.

Andra took his hand and squeezed it. The awe on her face made Kyro's heart skip a beat. Star Shepherding really could be wonderful.

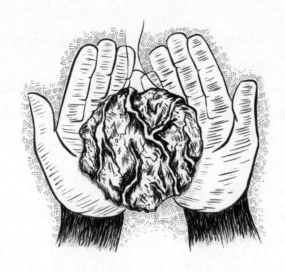

CHAPTER TEN

"NOW COMES THE FUN PART," KYRO SAID, LEADING
Andra back outside after checking through the window that the
vissla was gone. To his relief, it was nowhere in sight, and all
that it had left behind was melting ice. The only thing standing
in the yard was the catapult, illuminated by a single lamppost.
His father had rigged it so that its flame burned and snuffed
out like clockwork every evening, and tonight it lit their way
like a beacon.

"All Star Shepherds have catapults, but my father modified
this one with a few more gears and cogs to make it faster and
more accurate."

"The influence of his clockmaking skills again?" Andra said.

"Exactly." Kyro's smile fell. But he had more pressing matters at hand, like getting this star back into the sky before that vissla came back and found a way through the stardust barrier.

He placed the star into the sling.

"How does it work?" Andra asked.

Kyro pointed out what each part did. "First, you need to pull that lever there. Then when the red light stops blinking, hit this button here. That will launch the star. Would you like to do the honors?"

But before Andra could answer, a dark, hulking form lumbered through the trees. Kyro gasped, fearing for a moment that the vissla had returned.

The reality was just as bad.

"Andra! What are you doing? Get away from that infernal machine." Bodin stomped toward them, and Kyro wished he could curl up in the catapult and launch himself into the sky instead.

Andra went rigid. "Papa, I—"

Bodin cut her off, grabbing her arm and yanking her toward the village path. "You are in a world of trouble, young lady," he growled. "You are not to socialize with Star Shepherds."

He glowered at Kyro. "And you, boy, what do you think you're doing with my daughter?" He shoved his finger into Kyro's chest, and he shrank back against the catapult. Cypher barked and tugged at Bodin's pant leg, but the man shook him off.

"I'm sorry, I didn't mean—" Kyro began.

"Didn't mean what? To keep my daughter out all night? Where is your father? I'll give him a piece of my mind. You two fools have done more than enough damage to our village. I won't let you corrupt my daughter too."

"Papa!" Andra scowled. "I'm old enough to make up my own mind." She folded her arms across her chest.

Bodin's face turned so red, Kyro wouldn't have been surprised if he'd exploded right there in his yard. "Not while you're under my roof."

Andra clamped her mouth shut, her face nearly as crimson as her father's. Behind her, dawn crept over the mountains, swiftly encroaching on Kyro's sector of the sky.

Kyro's mouth suddenly went dry. "My father is missing. That's why I'm watching the stars tonight. I'm sorry, I didn't mean to keep her out late."

Bodin gave Kyro a grim look. "Don't come near my daughter again. Leave her and our village alone." He pulled Andra onto the path. She glanced back at Kyro and mouthed, *I'm sorry,* before the trees closed around their retreating figures.

The joy that had crept into Kyro's heart that evening faded like smoke on the wind. He picked up the star and loaded it into the catapult sling with heavy limbs. When he pressed the red

button, it beeped and some of the gears turned, but then they slowed to a grinding halt and black smoke coiled out of the base of the machine.

"Oh, no," Kyro whispered. "No, no, no."

He ran inside the workshop and grabbed his father's tools, desperately trying to remember how Tirin had fixed the catapult the last time it had broken down. Kyro opened the small door at the base and waved the billowing smoke away from his face. He tied an old handkerchief from his pocket over his nose, but he still coughed. Piece after piece, Kyro went through the guts of the catapult, but soon had no choice but to admit defeat. The machine was broken beyond his ability to fix. At least, before the dawn rose. He sagged against the catapult, head spinning.

Kyro managed to open the new case containing the star, wishing he could just hurl it into the sky in time. Hopelessness curled around his ankles, slowly working its way into his bones. He had protected it from falling into the hands of the vissla, but it didn't make a difference. He sank to the ground next to the star, and Cypher pawed at his knees.

As the light of dawn grew overhead, the star began to wane. Impulsively, Kyro cradled the star's heart in his hands. The idea of the star dying alone without its brothers and sisters was too much. He didn't even realize he was crying until Cypher began to lick the salt from his face.

The sun rose, its rays bursting over the sky. The molten star's light sputtered out, leaving only a gray rock cooling in Kyro's hands.

He had failed this star. He had failed his father, and his mother's memory. His father was right; he wasn't ready to watch the stars on his own after all.

CHAPTER ELEVEN

KYRO SPENT THE NEXT COUPLE OF DAYS IN A TERRIBLE funk. Every minute he had between eating, sleeping, and watching the night sky, he worked on the catapult. He had to fix it—and fast—or he wouldn't be able to save any stars. Two more had already been lost since the catapult broke.

Last night when a star had fallen, he'd raced from the tower, sprinting through the woods. Halfway to the star, a terrible wail shattered the peaceful night air. It had frozen Kyro in his tracks for a moment, then spurred him to move faster.

He was sure the sound was a vissla, dark and treacherous as it stalked the woods. He had to reach the star first. Even if he couldn't fix the catapult in time, he hated the thought of another star dying at a vissla's hands.

When he found the crater, the star and its soft ebbing light awaited him, and his relief was palpable. He grabbed it and took off. The keening in the woods nipped at his heels all the way to his yard, along with the familiar snap of cold.

Kyro's breath caught in his throat as he crossed the line of stardust and turned to face the vissla as it emerged from the tree line. The huge, shadowed creature writhed and screeched, as ice crept over the forest floor toward the yard, forming a silvery blanket that stopped right at the stardust. Cypher whined next to Kyro, gingerly shifting his feet because his paws were so cold.

A surge of terror and an undercurrent of pride coursed through Kyro's veins. He held the star in his hands aloft, and the vissla's screams pierced the night. The star's light seemed to grow and fill up the yard and forest, and Kyro threw up an arm to protect his eyes. Then the shadow creature let loose one last howl before the light consumed it.

The star returned to normal, but the vissla was gone. The icy blanket beneath his feet receded, melting into the leaves. Kyro could hardly believe it had worked.

That night, Kyro hadn't been able to send the star back into the sky, and it had fizzled out in his arms, but at least he had kept it out of the shadow's clutches. And the star had been able to do its job one last time before it was gone forever. That was some comfort, but not enough. It only fueled his determination to fix the catapult.

The next day as dusk began to fall, Kyro woke to a sharp rapping noise. Curious, he hurried to the front door, but found no one there. Only when he stepped outside did he notice the note taped to the door.

Kyro pulled it down, and his eyes raced over the words.

A meeting of the Star Shepherd Council will convene tomorrow at dusk at the Council's tower in Daluth to discuss Tirin's abandonment of his sacred duty to the stars over the village of Drenn. Tirin must appear before the Council to explain his actions, or he will be labeled a traitor and banned from shepherding the stars.

Kyro swallowed the words' bitter taste. His father was still missing. Not a single sign to let Kyro know he was alive. He had to believe his father was all right, but now even the Council had gotten wind of his disappearance.

Star Shepherding was the only thing his father loved; it was why he had left Drenn and his son behind, however foolishly. Kyro crumpled the note in his hand.

He was mad at his father, but the Council's declaration made him far angrier. He would have to go to Daluth in his father's place. Somehow, he must convince the Council to let Tirin remain a Star Shepherd.

The memory of his father at his mother's bedside flashed through his mind. He had been wrecked by her passing, and the stars were the only things that brought him any light. If he lost the stars too...

With renewed determination, Kyro threw open the door to the workshop, marched across the field, and set to work. The lamp his father had crafted to light up as the sun disappeared hummed behind him and illuminated his way. Furious energy tingled through his limbs as he crawled inside the huge catapult. He'd fix this machine, then head for the Council meeting tomorrow and show them everything was under control. He could even tell them he had captured a vissla. His father hadn't abandoned his post; he was chasing a lead while leaving the stars in his son's capable hands.

But Kyro needed to fix that catapult if he wanted to prove it.

This time he finally found the problem: a gear, buried deep in the inner workings, had come loose and was stuck at an awkward angle. He quickly freed the stuck, broken gear and set a new one into place, then sat back on his heels to examine his work. If his father were here, would he be proud? Tightness spread across his chest, and he scrambled out of the machine.

It didn't matter what his father might think; he wasn't here to see. He was off on some wild-goose chase, and Kyro was alone.

There was no one to help him now, not even the villagers—his father had seen to that.

Kyro took a deep breath, then closed the panel and dusted off his hands. Now to see if this worked.

He grabbed hold of the lever and yanked it down. The gears moving in unison sounded like music to Kyro's ears. When the red light blinked, he pressed the button and the catapult shot its imaginary cargo into the sky.

Relief flooded Kyro's bones. Cypher pawed his knee, and Kyro ran a hand through the dog's fur. "Let's go home, boy."

When he entered the workshop, he saw the crumpled note from the Council where he'd left it on the table, and the anger he'd felt earlier reared its head. How dare they question his father's devotion to the cause? It was his whole life.

Kyro threw the note in the fire. It sparked once, then burst into ashes.

He made his way up to the tower and settled into his father's chair. Cypher jumped up and licked his face, tail wagging. Kyro laughed despite himself.

"Down, boy." Cypher whined, then curled up on Kyro's lap to snooze.

Kyro had only been watching the stars in the cycling chair for an hour when someone knocked at the front door again. Could the Council members have changed their minds? Or did a new note await him downstairs? He set Cypher on the chair, the dog only lifting his head for a moment before returning to his dreams. When Kyro opened the door, his heart soared.

For a second time, Andra stood on his front steps.

"Hi." She waved. "Need any help watching the stars tonight?"

Her hopeful expression made Kyro's heart bounce against his ribs. He held the door wide to let her in, then frowned. "But your father—"

She placed a hand on Kyro's arm. "My father is wrong. And overprotective. *Your* father isn't even here. You shouldn't have to shoulder this responsibility alone. Not when you have friends willing to help."

His cheeks flushed, and he stammered, "Th-thank you."

Andra grinned and stepped inside. "I haven't been able to stop thinking about watching the stars."

Kyro tilted his head toward the tower. "Do you want a turn first?"

Her eyes widened. "Can I really?"

"Sure. But you'll have to kick Cypher out of the chair."

Andra laughed. "I don't mind sharing."

"Then you'll be his new best friend."

The dog had no qualms about curling up next to Andra. She set the chair in motion, and soon Cypher was fast asleep. Andra's eyes filled with delight as the chair took her from telescope to telescope, showing her every section of the sky.

"I'm always sleeping at night, and I never really considered how lovely the evening sky is before," Andra admitted. "But this is like a whole new world."

"If you look closely, you can see some of the stars grouped together. They're called constellations. I like to think they're families of people who gave a piece of their hearts to the stars together in the sky to keep us all safe." Kyro had never told this to anyone except his father.

"Inseparable families. That's so nice," Andra said.

A wave of sadness swept over Kyro. "Except now they're not as inseparable as they once were." He sank into a nearby chair, while Andra continued her watch.

"You keep watch every night," she said, leaning forward. "And you rescue the stars. It isn't your fault someone is stealing them."

He rubbed his palms on his knees. "I wish I was as good at clockmaking as my father. He never finished my training. When things break down here, I can't always fix them in time." The tightness from earlier crept back over his chest like a dark, vicious hand squeezing his breath.

"But that hasn't happened recently, has it?"

"The other night, just after your father took you home. The star we rescued... The catapult broke down, and I...I couldn't save it. I couldn't figure out what was wrong in time. I held it in my hands as its light faded." The backs of Kyro's eyes burned, and he looked away from Andra.

The chair stopped, and before Kyro knew it, she was at his side, flinging her arms around his neck.

"It isn't your fault," she whispered in his ear. "Your father shouldn't have left you alone. I think you're doing a fine job without him. Mistakes happen, and there are many more stars that you *have* saved and *will* save. You're doing wonderful work, Starboy."

Kyro didn't dare blink for fear that his eyes would overflow. He wondered if Andra knew how much he'd needed to hear her words.

She released him and squeezed his hand. "Let's take this next watch together."

Andra led Kyro back to the clockwork chair. It was big enough to fit both of them snugly, even with Cypher snoozing across their legs. The chair began to move, and they settled in for their watch.

Andra clung tightly to Kyro's hand, and he clung back. A glowing warmth filled him from his head to his toes, as though he were a star flying back to his own home in the sky.

CHAPTER TWELVE

KYRO AND ANDRA NESTLED IN THE CHAIR UNDER THE telescopes, keeping watch far into the night until the morning stretched its arms in the farthest corner of the sky. Soon the watch would be over and Andra would have to sneak back home before her father discovered she was missing.

But just as they had both resigned themselves to that idea, a brilliance lit the sky directly above the watchtower. They sat, frozen, as an entire constellation plummeted to the earth.

Andra gasped. Alarm flared over Kyro. How could they possibly transplant that many stars in the little time left before dawn?

He raced down the stairs, dragging Andra with him. Cypher lifted his head, curious, then went back to dreams of chasing mice. The pair burst out the door, and stopped short. The yard beyond the watchtower was dotted with a dozen smoking craters.

Empty smoking craters.

And yet not a single vissla was in sight, and the stardust circling the yard remained unbroken.

Kyro stumbled toward the nearest crater, reminded of that terrible night he and his father had discovered the stars were missing. It had happened again. But as Kyro waved away some of the smoke, something in the bottom of a crater caught his eye. He hopped down into it, and gingerly picked the thing up.

A severed hook.

Kyro sagged against the edge of the crater, cradling the hook in his hands. Andra dodged between all the other craters dotting the yard, but returned with hunched shoulders and a handful of hooks just like the one Kyro held. She sat next to him, her warmth doing nothing to stem the chill creeping over him.

Awful understanding slid through his gut. The slice through the burlap casings and now this severed hook. Kyro had never even seen one before. No one had, as far he knew. The Elders' magic had fixed the hooks in the sky, making them unshakable. They weren't ever supposed to fall.

Kyro's brain reeled, his breath suddenly short. The stars

weren't merely being stolen; they were being cut down. It was undeniable. Before, it could have been anything. The vissla, the villagers, the stars spontaneously combusting—but here was irrefutable proof. The hooks had been sliced off. Someone had done this on purpose.

And now all these stars were lost.

His father had only been gone a short while, and already Kyro was failing to keep up their Star Shepherding duties. The Council had maps of all the stars in the sky. His father had one of their sector hanging in his workshop. The missing constellation over the tower would forever mark them as failures. What would he tell the Council now? He hung his head and dizziness swept over him, the hook slipping from his fingers.

"All those stars," murmured Andra, her voice cracking. She wound her fingers through Kyro's hand. They watched, tears glimmering in their eyes, as dawn broke across the sky and the stars faded from view.

Wherever the fallen stars had ended up, it was too late for them now.

"Come on," Andra said, pulling Kyro up by his arm. "Let's get you inside."

He barely remembered Andra leading him into the house or how he stumbled the entire way. But when she sat him in a chair by the kitchen table and put a warm cup of cocoa in his hands, he began to return to himself.

"My father was right," Kyro said finally. "Someone *is* stealing the stars. They're cutting them down."

"But who would do such a thing? And how? Who could possibly get all the way up there?" Andra furrowed her brow.

"I don't know. I can't understand why anyone would want to do that. The villagers couldn't reach that far, and no one else lives near us, not for miles. The Elders used their mechanical giants to put them there in the first place, but those are long gone."

"Could it be those shadow creatures like we saw the other night?"

Kyro shook his head. "If it was, we'd hear the crackling of ice freezing over, we'd feel the cold lingering. It wasn't even a whole minute between when we saw them fall and us reaching the yard. Not even the vissla are that fast, and they don't seem to be able to get past the stardust protecting the yard. I think I was wrong about it being them."

Andra squeezed his hand, and he squeezed back. "Maybe your father's already on their trail. You said he went after whoever did this, right? He'll stop them. I'm sure of it."

Kyro wanted to scoff, but sipped from the mug of cocoa instead. The idea of his father following through on his promises seemed laughable...except when it had to do with the stars. That was the one thing he truly cared about. But where could his father have gone when the thief was still here in Drenn?

Kyro couldn't puzzle it out, but he knew his father would follow through if he could. No matter what happened to those left behind. Now Kyro had to answer for his father's absence.

"I don't know if he can. It's too much for one man. He should've gone to the Star Shepherd Council for help, but for some reason he chose not to."

"Why?" Andra frowned.

Kyro sighed. "He told them about the first star that was cut down on our watch, and heard rumors about the vissla there. I don't know why he wouldn't go back. But now I have to explain it."

"What do you mean?"

"The Council is putting my father on trial for abdicating his Star Shepherd duties. The meeting is tonight. If he doesn't show, he'll be labeled a traitor and banned from being a Star Shepherd." Kyro's eyes watered. No matter how much he resented Tirin's obsession with the stars, he couldn't let the Council take away the one thing that had given his father some small measure of hope.

"That's not fair." Andra said. "Your father only disappeared to save the stars."

Kyro shrugged. "Well, now I get to go in his place. Someone has to defend him to the Council."

Andra squeezed his hand again. "I could go with you. If you want. I've seen how dedicated he is to his job."

"I don't want to drag you into this." Kyro ducked his head. "Your father hates me enough as it is, and I'd feel terrible if you got into trouble again because of me. You're risking enough just being here now."

Andra was quiet for several moments. "When must you leave?"

"This morning." Kyro placed his empty mug on the table. He dreaded making this trip. He'd have to tell the Council of his failures and all the stars that fell last night. And in the process, he'd be leaving this section of the sky unwatched.

"I'll help you pack." She stood and stretched. "I'm not ready to go home yet."

While Kyro stuffed a satchel with essentials and the map to the Council's tower that his father kept in a workshop drawer, Andra put together some of the food from the groceries she'd brought over. When Kyro returned from his bedroom, he saw the little paper bag that contained the sweets and couldn't help but smile.

He hoisted his pack onto his shoulder, called Cypher to him, and took one last look around the house. An odd feeling struck Kyro. He'd only be gone for a day or two, but the idea of leaving caused an unexpected lump to form in the back of his throat.

"Let me walk you home," Kyro said. Cypher wagged his tail at the prospect of going for a walk.

Together they headed toward the village. They didn't say

a word as they wove through the craters dotting Kyro's yard. Each were lost in their own thoughts, the sounds of their foot-falls punctuated by birds singing and insects humming in the forest. And each of their hearts was a little heavier than it had been the night before.

When they reached the village gates, Andra turned to Kyro. "Good luck with the Council. Don't worry about the stars here," she said. "You've shown me how to send them back to the sky. I'll be watching them while you're gone."

"No, Andra, it's too dangerous. The vissla—"

She put a finger to his lips. "The vissla won't be able to catch me. Go and defend your father, Starboy, and don't worry about Drenn."

She grinned, then stepped through the gates. Kyro watched her retreating form march toward the sun rising over the roof-tops until she disappeared from view. Then he took a deep breath and headed back into the woods.

CHAPTER THIRTEEN

TIRIN HAD NEVER TAKEN KYRO WITH HIM TO THE STAR Shepherd meetings in the past. He went to their main watchtower in Daluth twice a year to report to the Council, and from what he had told Kyro, it was a long trek that would take him almost an entire day to complete if he went on foot.

That was why his father had crafted a mechanical clockwork cart, large enough to hold a grown man. Or, in this case, a boy and his dog. The cart was something his father had invented, as far as Kyro knew. He had heard of new ships that used clockwork steering and rigging to control the sails, but that was only beginning to become popular.

Kyro left the village behind and returned to the watchtower, heading around to a shed in the back that his father rarely touched nowadays. He was grateful that his father hadn't thought to take the cart with him, though that worried him too.

He opened the shed door and pulled the covering off the cart. It was a clunky thing, but functional, and moved on rollers with the help of his father's innovative clockmaking. The brass gears gleamed in the morning light. His father always cleaned it to a shine when he returned from traveling across the Black Lands. Kyro would have to remember to do the same.

He tossed his pack inside and whistled for Cypher. The dog poked his snout around the edge of the shed door, then bounded to Kyro's side.

He clambered into the cart, tugging Cypher in after him, then pulled out the map his father always took with him on the journey to the Council's watchtower. Tirin had left it behind, stuffed in the drawer of his workbench. Wherever he had gone, it wasn't there.

Kyro examined the folded parchment. It took a moment for him to get his bearings on the map, but when he did, he frowned. He was going to have to cross the Black Lands. The other option was to sail over the Pegian Sea, but that was impossible without a boat and a much longer journey. He shivered. He'd heard the heat of the Black Lands alone was enough to disorient people, making it easy to get lost and wander the desert forever.

But that had never happened to his father, and it wouldn't happen to Kyro either. He knew the sky well; even though there were no stars out now, he could judge direction from the position of the sun. The sky was the one thing he could depend on to always remain the same. At least until someone had decided to start chopping down the stars.

But no one had taken the sun, and that was something.

Kyro gave Cypher a snack and a pat on the head. "It's going to be a long day," he said.

He pulled the lever next to him, waited for the whistle to sound, and then pressed the button to start the gears rolling. He steered the cart from the shed using a shifting lever on his right. It stuttered at first, but once Kyro got the hang of how to navigate, he angled the cart toward the woods.

The map took them on a path that Kyro had glimpsed once or twice, but never taken before. The cart chugged along for the better part of an hour before the spindly trees Kyro knew so well began to thin out. They were replaced by scrub and brush and fields of flowers. But as the day went on, the flowers disappeared from the fields and turned into thinning grasses and low bushes. The dirt beneath the cart began to darken, coating the rollers as black as soot.

The temperature rose, and as it did, Kyro shed his jacket and stuffed it in his pack. By midmorning, they reached the edge of the Black Lands, and he stopped the cart to stretch his legs and share some water with Cypher. The blackened sands unfolded before him as far as he could see. The dunes rose and fell, dotted here and there with petrified trees, reaching toward the sky as though they were struggling to breathe over the black waves. Kyro's resolve faltered.

Had this place once been more like the forest he knew at Drenn? What had happened to kill everything and turn it to ashy sand?

Cypher whined beside him, and Kyro sighed. "I don't want to go in there either. But I think we have to. We must get to the Council's watchtower before nightfall."

After one more drink of water, the pair got back into the cart and set off into the shifting dunes.

Only mere minutes passed before Kyro understood how someone could get lost in the Black Lands. Everything was dark, yet glinting from the sun overhead. It was confusing to the senses. The Black Lands seemed endless.

Kyro checked his positioning by the map and the sun at regular intervals as the cart trundled along, the watch on his wrist counting down the minutes until the Council meeting. Here and there, giant pieces of structures and old lumber from abandoned carts stuck out from the sands. Despite their chilling appearance, they were proof he was getting somewhere and not wandering in circles.

The sun had climbed far into the sky and was beginning its

journey to the west when Kyro heard the sound that made his stomach drop.

Crrrrreeakkkkk...clunk.

The cart faltered to a stop, smoke and dust curling from its underbelly. Kyro yanked at his unruly hair.

This can't break down too, he thought. *Not now!*

He scrambled free of the cart and peered at the gears clogging the underside. What he saw made him sink back on his heels.

A hook—severed just like the ones he'd seen the night before—had gotten caught in the roller's gears, piercing one of the cogs and causing another to be bent too far to be saved. Kyro already knew the damage to the skies was not confined to their territory, but the proof was jarring nonetheless.

Kyro had thought to bring his father's tools, but he hadn't had the time or space to bring spare parts. His shoulders slumped. He had no choice but to abandon the cart. His father would be furious. Still, perhaps his father could eventually come back for the cart and fix it later. It wasn't like this was a well-traveled route, though the sand did seem to swallow everything. Kyro removed the star hook from the cogs and tucked it in his bag. It seemed wrong to leave it behind.

He stood and pulled Cypher out of the cart too. Desperation curled around Kyro's legs, but when Cypher licked his face, he gave a half-hearted laugh. "Sorry, boy, it looks like it's going to be a long walk after all."

He shouldered his pack and set out on foot, all the while trying to escape the gnawing worry.

They had walked for nearly an hour when they had to stop again to rest. Kyro paused under one of the largest sunken structures they'd seen. It looked like a house had been sliced in two, and one half had been buried under the sands. He found a place to sit under a bit of shade. Cypher panted, his tongue lolling out of the side of his mouth.

"Here, buddy, have some water," Kyro said, pouring some from his canteen into a small bowl he'd brought along. Cypher lapped it up, then curled up by his master's side and began to snooze. Kyro checked his watch.

At the pace they were traveling, he'd have to present his case to the Council in these dirty clothes. There would be no time to clean up or change beforehand, even if they did rest for a few minutes.

Kyro's feet ached, and he unlaced his boots to dump out the sand that had been chafing at them for the last few miles. He sighed in relief as air curled between his toes. He set his shoes to the side and rested his head back against the petrified structure. He'd only close his eyes for a moment, then they'd be on their way again…

A loud yelp startled Kyro awake. He leapt to his feet when he realized Cypher was no longer next to him. The yelp sounded again, and Kyro's heart twisted.

He ran into the sands, barefoot, calling for his dog.

"Cypher! Here, boy! Where are you?"

He adjusted his path at another yelp, this one more strangled than the last, and circled around to the other side of the structure.

The petrified wood stuck out of a low dune, and there was Cypher in the center.

Slowly sinking.

The dog's nose and front paws were still above the sands, frantically scraping at the edge of the quicksand pit. Kyro's stomach clenched. He couldn't let anything happen to Cypher; the dog was all he had left of his family.

He grabbed the nearest petrified branch and stretched it out over the pit. Cypher struggled harder, but couldn't reach the branch. Fear gripped Kyro.

He slipped off his pack and pulled out the blanket he'd brought. He stepped as close as he dared to the edge of the quicksand and tossed the blanket out. The sands had reached Cypher's front legs, but he managed to keep them free. On Kyro's fifth attempt to reach him with the blanket, Cypher's teeth clamped down on the edge.

Kyro tugged hard, and Cypher began to break free of the sand trap. Hand over hand, Kyro pulled the blanket closer. When Cypher was at last secure in his arms, joyfully licking his face, Kyro scrambled to the other, safer side of the sunken structure, then collapsed against it. They were both covered in black sand, but Kyro didn't care. He squeezed Cypher tightly, and the dog didn't even squirm.

He'd be a mess when he saw the Council, but at least they'd both make it there alive.

"We've got to hurry now." Kyro secured Cypher's leash around his neck, just in case they encountered any more of the sand traps.

They trekked onward, the black earth beneath them churning. It wasn't long before they both looked as though they had rolled around in a chimney. The farther they walked, the more exhausted they became. But Kyro knew they had no choice; stopping now would be the most dangerous thing they could do. It felt as though they were surrounded by darkness, despite the sun overhead. Kyro did his best not to think of the stories his mother had told him about the dangers that lurked in the Black Lands.

It was well into the afternoon when Kyro heard an odd sound. Something metallic and scraping and getting closer. His heart sped up, but when he glanced around, he saw nothing but black sand for miles.

Kyro took one more step, and the sand beneath his feet erupted. A huge, insect-like creature burst from the black dunes, legs flailing. Kyro stumbled back, Cypher yapping bravely in front of him as the beast landed on its incessantly moving legs. It was the color of night, blending in with the sands. It had too

many appendages to count, all of which appeared to be razor sharp, and huge clacking pincers. It opened its maw and let out an earsplitting scream, then lunged toward them. Kyro ducked to the side, narrowly avoiding one of the terrible pincers, then jumped out of the way of the thing's tail.

Kyro eyed the beast warily as it circled back around. Could this be another of the shadow creatures from his mother's stories? There were so many kinds that he didn't remember them all. He shuddered.

The great creature lunged at him again, but this time Kyro was ready. He tossed the star hook that had ruined the cart in the direction they came from, hoping to create a distraction. The beast took the bait. It leapt up after the hook, and when it failed to catch it in its pincer, it threw itself into the chase.

Kyro and Cypher ran for their lives, wanting nothing more than to leave this terrible wasteland behind. But there was nowhere to run from the creature. Just shadowy dunes as far as the eye could see, with the occasional debris. They ducked behind the first thing they could find: a huge petrified log that looked like it might have once been an old-growth tree. Kyro clutched Cypher to his chest, and they both held their breath.

The clacking sound of the insect got closer. It must have lost interest in the hook. Kyro squeezed his eyes closed, shivering even against the warmth of his dog. He could hear the giant shadow insect behind them, every *click-clack* of its pincers and legs like drumbeats.

Then he heard a new sound. Sands shifting. The wake of it pushed them and the log they hid behind all the way down the dune. For a full minute Kyro and Cypher sat there, waiting in torturous silence.

But they didn't hear the sound of the beast again, and when Kyro grew brave enough to peek over the log, it was nowhere in sight. It must have returned to its lair under the sands. Strange that it would venture out during the day. The dark creatures were getting bolder after the loss of the stars. Perhaps the darkness of the Black Lands lent them some protection too.

Kyro stood on wobbling legs and took a deep breath. Then they headed out once again. For the rest of the journey, they were on high alert, constantly searching for threats. Kyro wasn't sure what would happen with the Council, but there was one thing he knew for certain: he would never, ever travel here again.

It was late in the afternoon when the two of them stood filled with relief at the edge of the Black Lands, a field of rough scrub and brush stretching out between them and a vast ocean.

Not far away, at the top of a cliff overlooking the sea, stood a giant watchtower.

Even from this distance, it was clearly many times larger than the tower Kyro called home. The number of telescopes

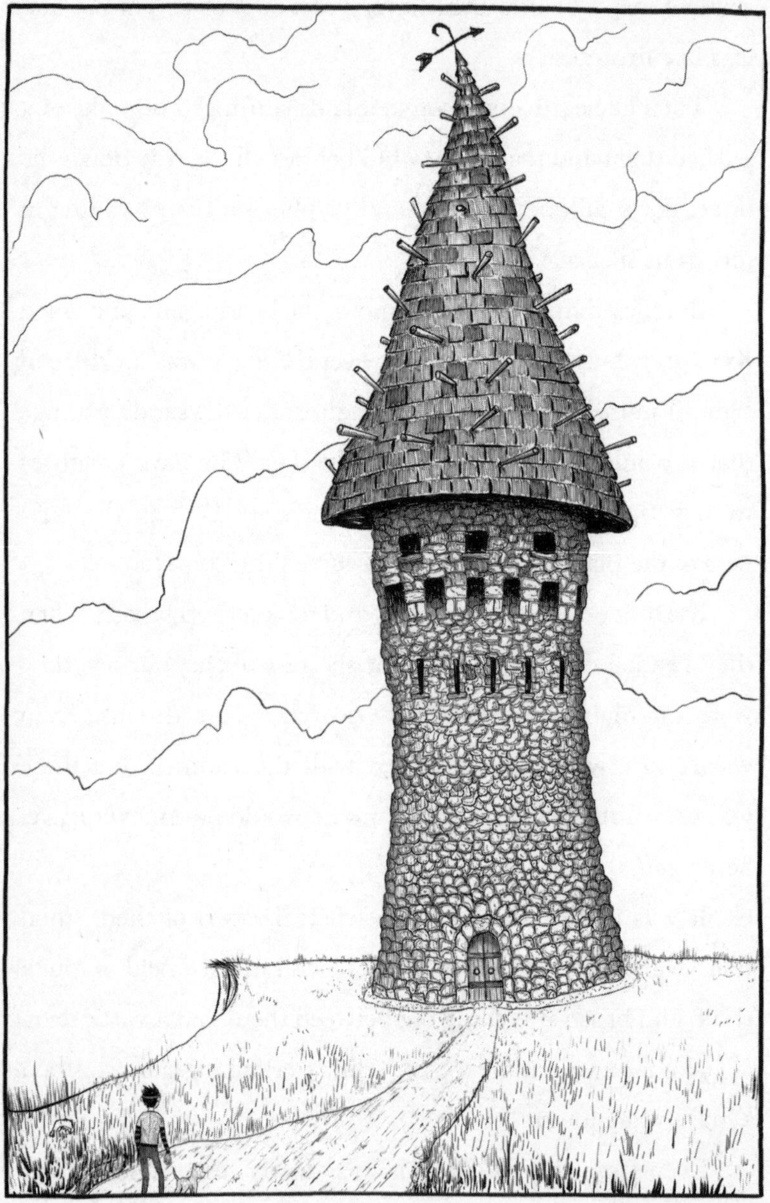

dotting the expansive roof must have taken several Star Shepherds to man every night.

A thrill jolted through Kyro. They'd made it. And if he hadn't been here under such unpleasant circumstances, he would have been impressed. The stars they must be able to see from there! With the ocean next to them, the entire world could be viewed from that one spot on the cliff.

But Kyro was here for his father this time, not to wonder at the stars. He dusted off Cypher and his own clothes the best he could, and then they hurried across the field to plead his father's case.

CHAPTER FOURTEEN

BY THE TIME KYRO AND CYPHER REACHED THE TOP OF the cliff and the entrance to the Council's magnificent watchtower, they were exhausted. Kyro could barely lift the brass knocker on the door, but somehow he managed. The sound reverberated through his bones. He wished to sleep, but nervous energy filled him from the tips of his ears down to his toes.

The heavy wooden door creaked open, and an imposing man with a shaved head and close-cut beard stood in their path. His arms were more tanned than those of the sailors Kyro had seen occasionally in Drenn, and he folded them as he looked at Kyro expectantly. The boy's mouth hung open. He wasn't sure what he had expected the other Star Shepherds to be like, but it wasn't this. Except the intimidating part, of course. That much he had gathered from the note that had been pinned to his door.

"H-hello," Kyro stammered. "I'm here for the Star Shepherd Council meeting."

The man raised an eyebrow. "Aren't you a little young?"

Kyro's cheeks flamed. "No, sir. My father and I man our watchtower together."

"And where is your father?"

Good question. "He wasn't able to make it."

The man considered Kyro for a moment longer, his eyes roving over the dirty dog at his side. Cypher sat up straight, tail wagging, on his best behavior.

"All right," the man said, moving aside to let Kyro enter. "Where is your assigned region?" He picked up a clipboard from a nearby table.

"Drenn, sir. Our watchtower is just outside the village of Drenn."

The man's brows knit together; then his dark eyes widened. "Drenn, huh? No wonder your father isn't able to make it to the meeting. It's a shame."

Kyro hung his head, but heat burned inside him.

"I'm Jakris," the man said, holding out a hand for Kyro to shake. "Since I know you're not Tirin, what is your name for the registry?"

Kyro shook the man's hand. "My name is Kyro."

"Well, Kyro, keep your chin up. Tell the truth about your father, and the Council may be persuaded to be lenient."

The knot in his stomach loosened. Perhaps Jakris wasn't so bad after all. "Thank you, sir."

"Just Jakris, please. Now, come along. The Council is ready. A few more stragglers might show up, but you may as well go in and get it over with."

Jakris ushered Kyro and Cypher through a hall that wound around the watchtower, slowly working its way into the bedrock of the cliff. Doors to each level dotted the sides of the hall, and Kyro imagined the rooms beyond must be full of finery and instruments to send the stars back where they belonged in the sky.

Along the walls of the hall were paintings and plaques. The paintings were night scenes featuring magnificent watchtowers. Titles like *The Tower of Peliana* and *The Spire of Spinto* and *The Keep of Ergal* were engraved on the elegant frames. The watchtowers depicted in the paintings were all finely crafted, and over their roofs hung a sky of sparkling stars. Between the paintings hung plaques with names of Star Shepherds, the dates they'd kept their watch, and the number of stars they'd rescued over the course of their careers.

Kyro's heart climbed into his throat. His father must have seen this hall and these plaques many times. No doubt, he wished to find his own name among them some day. Kyro's mouth went dry. If he wasn't successful with the Council, his father never would.

He tried not to look, but he couldn't help watching the names go by. Suddenly, he stopped and placed his hand on the wall next to one particular plaque: Jax and Yanna of the Romvi Watchtower. Those were his grandparents' names. They had passed away when he was very young. And they had lived in a tower by Romvi, the village where Kyro was born.

"Someone you know?" Jakris asked.

Kyro dropped his hand to his side. "I think those are my grandparents."

"I believe it. There are many generations in these halls."

The longer they walked, the slicker Kyro's palms grew. Would his name ever be on one of these plaques? Did he want it to be? He went over the words he needed to say to the Council, and hoped he'd remember them all when he was in a room full of people staring down at him.

He swallowed hard and shoved his hands into his pockets.

Jakris stopped before a large oaken door, but he paused before pulling the latch.

"You might want to leave your dog here."

Kyro bent down to Cypher. "Be a good boy, and wait out here for me. Stay." He scratched between the dog's ears, and though Cypher whined when Kyro stood up, he remained seated.

"Ready?" Jakris asked.

"As I'll ever be," Kyro said.

Jakris laughed. "Good luck. There are those present who know your father and respect him. Don't forget that."

Kyro stared in surprise, but Jakris didn't notice as he opened the door. The hall was packed wall to wall and level over level with men and women from many different walks of life, representing regions all over the world. A platform stood in the center of the circular room with a chair that could rise and fall to address different levels of the tall hall. It was descending at the moment, carrying a thin man with a gray beard and sharp green eyes who addressed the crowd.

"That's Kadmos, the leader of the Council," Jakris whispered. Then he nudged Kyro forward.

Kadmos finished his introductory speech and alighted on the main floor. He took in Kyro's appearance with a look of distaste.

"Who are you?" he asked.

Jakris stepped forward. "This is Kyro, of the Drenn watchtower. He's here on behalf of his father, Tirin."

Kadmos scowled and folded his hands in front of his midnight-blue robes. Kyro noticed that everyone—even Jakris—wore the same robes. He wanted to shrink into the floor. Was there a Star Shepherd dress code? His father had never told him about it, like so many other things.

"Where is your father, Kyro?" Kadmos asked, and the room around them began to buzz. "Why didn't he come on his own?"

Kyro took a deep breath. "He is not at home at present. He is—"

"You mean he abandoned his post? The rumors we've been hearing out of Drenn are true?" Kadmos's eyes glinted.

"He did not abandon anything. He—"

"Then why is he not here?" Kadmos stepped closer to Kyro. "He is the only approved Star Shepherd assigned to watch the skies over Drenn. If he is not watching them, then he has abandoned his post." A terrible sort of smile slid over Kadmos's face. "Tirin is a traitor."

A ripple of murmurs flared all the way up into the heights of the tower. The sound that echoed back down to Kyro was nearly deafening.

"He is *not* a traitor!" Kyro shouted. The Council grew quiet, and he instantly regretted raising his voice, but there was no help for it now.

"Then by all means," Kadmos stretched his hands out. "Answer the question. Where is Tirin?"

Heat flashed over Kyro's face, and a trickle of sweat trailed down his back. "He came here not long ago to report strange slices in some of the burlap cases. While he was here, he heard other rumors about the vissla returning and stars going astray in other sectors."

"Yes, yes, we know all this. We were here," Kadmos said, gesturing to the Council members. "And those 'reports' as you call them were shaky at best."

Kyro took a deep breath. "After he returned, we made an even more frightening discovery. One night, a cluster of stars fell over the Radamak Mountains."

"Which, might I remind you, are forbidden," Kadmos said.

"I know, and we were saddened to lose those stars. Later the same night, another cluster fell outside of Drenn. We rushed to save them, but when we got there, all we found were empty craters. Someone *took* the stars—every last one of them. To make matters worse, I can confirm that the vissla are indeed back. I've encountered them at least three times over the last few weeks. I even destroyed one. They're terrifying. The legends are true; stars can ward them off when wielded against them, but if they get their hands on a star first, they kill it."

Audible gasps rang out. "Impossible!" reverberated throughout the hall.

Kadmos laughed. "*Destroyed* a vissla?" He shook his head. "Do you really expect us to believe that? Your imagination is just as formidable as your father's."

"It's the truth. I swear it."

A smattering of laughter trickled down above Kyro's head, and his face reddened.

"Of course you did," Kadmos said. "Please, continue your explanation of your father's disappearance."

Kyro swallowed the sand lining his throat. "After that night, my father knew someone was taking the stars. He went after them. To catch them. To stop them. But that's not all. Since then, I've discovered someone isn't just taking the stars; someone is cutting them down. See?"

He pulled one of the severed hooks left in the craters the night before from his pack. The Council went deadly silent.

"At first I thought it had to be the vissla, but the night I found this, several stars had fallen above our watchtower, and in the mere time it took for me to run outside, they were gone," Kyro said.

"A fine tale, to be sure," Kadmos said. "But have you anyone to vouch for this story? If you are the only witness to this, how do we know you aren't making it all up out of affection for your father?"

Kyro's hands squeezed into fists. "My father is out there, alone, trying to save the stars because you wouldn't listen to him when he came here the first time!"

"Do you know how many times Tirin has come to our Council meetings, filled with false stories and conspiracies?" Kadmos huffed. "The first few times we took him seriously and investigated, only to have it turn out to be all in his head. You are just like your traitor father."

Heat flared over Kyro's cheeks. He had never heard about this before. He barely kept his tongue in check.

"You have no one to vouch for this story, do you?" Kadmos said. A whisper of *traitor* breathed through the gathered Council members until it roared in Kyro's ears.

Jakris placed his hands on Kyro's shoulders, startling him. "I believe him. I know Tirin has tried the Council's patience in the past, but this time, several of us have seen strange things too. And I've seen the vissla myself. They are all too real. If someone is cutting down the stars, we should send people after Tirin to help him. He's a hero, not a traitor."

Kadmos scoffed. "A hero? How many stars have died since Tirin left, boy?"

Kyro froze. This was the one question he had been dreading. The one thing he had prayed they would not ask.

But lying wouldn't help him. Kadmos had the look of a predator that knew its prey was caught. Kyro was willing to bet that the Council leader already knew the answer.

"Fifteen," Kyro whispered. "There were fifteen I could not save. Our catapult broke down, and—"

"Fifteen stars, lost for eternity." Kadmos raised his arms and returned to his chair. "Fifteen stars that we swore to protect and that were lost because your father abandoned his post."

"No, it wasn't his fault, it was mine. I couldn't fix the catapult in time for the first few, then last night a dozen fell all at once, and those were stolen before I could get to them."

"A likely story, I'm sure. Your catapult has been modified beyond standard specifications by your father, yes?"

Kyro's heart sunk into his feet. "Yes, sir."

"Well, then. I think it is time for a vote." Kadmos pressed a button on the chair, and it shot up to the highest level. "Tier 9, how do you judge Tirin?" His voice jangled Kyro's bones.

One by one, Kyro saw the specks of their voting paddles turn. Every one of them was black. Jakris squeezed his shoulders.

A man who must be the Council secretary scurried around below and recorded the vote of each tier as Kadmos progressed. "Tier 8, how do you judge Tirin?"

This time, there were two white voting paddles in a sea of black. Small hope flared in Kyro's heart. It was soon dampened by the votes of the next two tiers. Then again, a spot of white at the fifth tier. But the last four were the same: black, black, black, black. The lone vote with a white paddle on the first tier was Jakris, who had remained at Kyro's side. The verdict was clear before Kadmos's chair even touched the floor.

Guilty.

Kadmos allowed the secretary to finish counting the votes, though it was only for show. When there was an official tally, Kadmos smiled.

"The Council hereby declares Tirin of Drenn guilty of abandoning his post as Star Shepherd."

"This is wrong!" Kyro cried. "He was only trying to help." Jakris put a hand on Kyro's arm to keep him from doing anything rash.

"I am afraid you failed to prove that," Kadmos said.

"I'll find proof. I'll clear his name. I swear I can!" Kyro tried unsuccessfully to shake off Jakris's strong grip.

"Until you do," Kadmos said, "your territory will be divided up between the Shepherds in neighboring regions." He licked his lips before uttering the words that nearly made Kyro's heart thud to a stop. "And you're both banned from touching the stars."

CHAPTER FIFTEEN

KYRO LEFT THE COUNCIL'S WATCHTOWER AT DUSK
with his pack, his dog, and assurances from Jakris that he'd
try to persuade the Council to be more reasonable. Since they
had decided it would be more prudent to divide the coverage between neighboring Shepherds than to send a replacement immediately, Kyro's tower wouldn't have a new occupant
until they went through the approval process for a new Star
Shepherd. According to Jakris, they didn't get that many appli-
cants anymore, and it would likely be months before they
appointed a replacement.

Even so, any hope he had been harboring that his father

might be redeemed had fled. The Council had even taken back Kyro's starglass goggles to ensure he couldn't find the stars so easily if he was tempted to disobey them. It still hadn't really sunk in that he'd been banned from touching the stars. He feared the weak hollowness inside him was only an echo of what was to come.

Night was upon them, and now Kyro would have to find a place to sleep or head back home. He couldn't stand the thought of staying in Daluth for a second longer than necessary after how the Council had treated his father.

Yet, the thought of treading over the Black Lands with its sand traps and dangerous creatures again—especially at night—was a thing Kyro dreaded. His stomach clenched at the memory of Cypher struggling to paw his way free of the quicksand and the enormous creature with many razored legs. There was a port town below the cliff and the watchtower. Perhaps they might have a suggestion of a better means of getting home. Kyro had heard from his father that the sea passage was safer and shorter than going through the Black Lands, but it was also very expensive. They'd never had the extra money to try it.

They headed down the hill and slipped into the town unnoticed. At the first trough he could find, Kyro washed off his face and hands and Cypher as best he could. The black, sooty sand still clung to them, but the cool water made them both marginally more presentable. If Kyro wanted to find help here, he'd better not look like a thieving street urchin.

The port town was small, but clearly hadn't suffered for it. It bustled with activity, from the manor houses up on the hill all the way to the taverns and merchant shops and down to the docks. The air was salty with sea brine, which almost reminded him of home. Drenn had a much smaller port than this place, but that salty air was unmistakable.

A few travelers or townspeople—it was impossible to tell which—gave Kyro strange glances, but most ignored him and went on their way. He could be invisible here. No one knew who he was. This filled Kyro with a mix of power and sadness. He was someone; he just wasn't someone here.

As he ventured through the merchant shops, a sweet smell, like chocolate croissants baked to a perfect golden brown, wafted over to him. He missed Andra. Her soft hands and laughing voice, and how she always smelled as sweet as the pastries in the bakery.

He wondered if she really was sneaking out at night to keep watch in the tower. Or if she'd been caught by Bodin and gotten into trouble already. He hoped not, for both their sakes and the stars'.

Kyro's stomach growled as he made his way down to the docks. Perhaps he could convince someone to let him work on a ship that would take him back to Drenn. He found an empty overturned crate and shooed away the gulls before sitting down and opening his pack. He pulled out some jerky for himself and a couple biscuits for Cypher, and they ate their meal while they watched the gulls swoop and dive into the bay.

Sailors and shipboys scurried across the docks. One group caught Kyro's eye as they wandered from a nearby tavern and strolled back toward the big ships moored at the end of the docks. They joked and shoved each other. Their laughter rang through the air, making Kyro's heart hurt. He didn't have anyone to laugh with, unless you counted Cypher.

He began to turn away, but a word caught his attention: Drenn.

"Hurry up, boys!" one sailor yelled trotting down the dock ahead of the others. "Captain will be furious if we're late shipping out for Drenn! We can't spend long there as it is, since we have to continue on to Sanforia."

Kyro nearly dropped his lunch. He leapt up and ran toward the sailors.

"Excuse me?" he called. They swung around, and one of them laughed.

"Yes?" the sailor said. He was a young man with sun-weathered skin and a ring piercing his nose.

"Are you in need of help on your ship? I can do odd jobs and wash floors."

The group laughed. "Sorry, mate, but we've already got a shipboy. If you want passage, you'll have to pay the captain."

Kyro trailed after the group as they returned to the ship, hoping to think of something, anything, he could say that might make them change their minds.

Nothing came to him, but he did see the ship they boarded. It was a large steamship that ran on coal and had new clockwork rigging for the sails. His father would have loved to see this, he was sure. A fascinating system of ropes, pulleys, chains, and cogs controlled the sails all from a single panel of buttons in the ship's bridge. There was no need for the extra manual labor like on other ships, but the rigging was very expensive. Chances were that a ticket to board this ship would be expensive too.

Kyro's heart sunk as he put his hand in his pack and ran his fingers over the two small coins at the bottom. That was all they had left of their last stipend from the Star Shepherd Council, which would be cut off now that they were banned from watching the stars. No way could he afford a real ticket.

His stomach growled again, the meager meal he had just eaten already souring in his gut. There was some food left in the cabinets of his home. If he could even go home. What if the Council had already sent someone to lock up their tower?

Kyro shook off his fears and made up his mind. He couldn't risk the Black Lands again without a working cart, and he couldn't pay for a ticket. He hated to do it, but he was going to have to stow away on a ship, and pray he didn't get caught.

Kyro and Cypher strolled as casually as they could up and down the docks, watching the ships and hanging around long enough to discern their destinations. The ship those sailors he'd spoken to earlier worked on was the only one headed to Drenn. Now Kyro just had to figure out how to get in one of the crates they were loading onto the ship.

He sat down by the trough where they'd eaten earlier and was considering his options when he spied a familiar tall figure haggling with a fishmonger further down the docks.

Suddenly Kyro knew exactly what to do. After all, Jakris had told him he wanted to help.

He approached Jakris just as he turned away from the fishmonger, swinging a couple silver fish strung on a small pole. Surprise ran over Jakris's face.

"Kyro, why aren't you on your way home?"

Kyro kicked at a rock stuck between the boards.

"Remember when you said you wished you could help?" He smiled hopefully.

Jakris studied Kyro for a moment. "The Council would censure me if I paid your way on a ship so soon after you've been cast out of our ranks."

"Oh, no, I wouldn't dream of asking you to pay my way. But do they have any rules about causing a little distraction?"

Jakris's eyes widened. "What do you need a distraction for?"

Kyro grinned, trying to exude more confidence than he felt, even though his stomach twisted. "So I can sneak on board. I can't go across the Black Lands again. I almost lost my dog on the way here."

Jakris laughed. "You are very different than your father, Kyro." He paused, then sighed. "All right, I shall help you. There are no rules against that."

Relief flooded Kyro. "Thank you. Cypher and I will walk past that ship over there"—he pointed to the one headed for Drenn—"and then we'll double back and duck down behind those crates waiting to be loaded into the hull. If you can distract the sailors, then we can crawl inside one of the crates."

"All right," Jakris said with a wink. "This might actually be fun. Definitely more than the Council."

Kyro picked up his things, Cypher at his heels. His heart drummed against his rib cage as he neared the big ship. A thousand questions swam through his brain. If he was caught, what would they do to him? What if the sailors on the docks noticed him doubling back? What if he got into the wrong crate and ended up on the wrong ship? What if Jakris was terrible at causing distractions? Or worse, what if he told on him?

He walked past the steamer and then another ship, a schooner, before doubling back and ducking down behind one of the large shipping crates. Next to the ship was a giant pulley and a platform that rose and fell using gears as big as Kyro himself. He held his breath, hoping Jakris was true to his word and gave him the opening he would need to get safely inside the crate with Cypher.

A few moments later, Jakris's tall shadow fell over the nearby sailors.

"Hey!" Jakris yelled. "I know you. You cheated me out of a hundred gold pieces at cards last week." Kyro peeked around the crate to see Jakris, in all his intimidating glory, shoving his finger into one of the sailor's chests. The sailor's friends came to his defense.

"You've got the wrong man, mate! We were aboard *The Celestine* down near Peliana last week."

"Oh, I don't think so," Jakris growled. "I never forget a face."

All the sailors had their backs to Kyro. This was his chance. He scooped up Cypher and opened the lid of the crate as quietly as he could. He peeked inside. It was filled with straw and a few large pieces of wood and planks. Probably destined for the woodworker in the Drenn marketplace. Kyro hopped inside and nestled into the hay between the pieces, then closed the lid of the crate. The latch caught automatically.

Outside, Jakris wrapped up his ploy.

"Really? You're sure you weren't in this port?"

"Yes, for the last time. Now go away and let us do our jobs."

"You got a brother?" he asked.

"No!"

Jakris mumbled something else, and then, through a crack in the crate, Kyro watched him walk back toward the town.

Kyro sighed. Now all he had to do was wait.

CHAPTER SIXTEEN

KYRO AND CYPHER HUDDLED TOGETHER IN THE CRATE, the sky above growing darker, while they waited for it to be loaded into the hull of the steamship. At first, fear of discovery kept them alert, but eventually they dozed off.

They were jolted awake by the crate bumping and moving. Kyro bit his tongue and clung to Cypher.

"I swear these things get heavier as the day goes on," one of the sailors complained.

"That's 'cause you're a weakling," another said, and several voices joined in the laughter.

The crate jolted and lurched until it hit the floor inside the cargo hold. Voices shouted, and someone patted the crate with a heavy hand. It reverberated all the way to Kyro's teeth.

"That's the last of them," said a sailor nearby. "Tell the captain we're ready to raise anchor."

Footsteps ran up the stairs, but another man pattered around the hold for a while longer. Every step echoed back to Kyro, scraping against his nerves. He wrapped his arms around his knees and remained as still as he possibly could. To his relief, Cypher soon fell asleep next to him. One less thing to worry about.

Now all he had to do was wait it out until they docked in Drenn. Then they could sneak off this ship and go home to the watchtower.

Hopefully, it would be easier than the rest of their trip had been.

✂ ✄

Kyro fell asleep just before the ship departed, but when he woke up a few hours later, he began to wonder if the ocean might be worse than the Black Lands after all. He'd never been on a boat before. His father only left his tower when he had to visit the Council, and Kyro didn't go farther than the docks in Drenn.

But he weathered the swaying and dipping and the drops in his stomach the best he could. When the ship hit a rough patch, his gut lurched into his throat. Kyro tried valiantly to hold it in, but it was too much. He retched in a corner of the container and accidentally woke up Cypher. The dog let out a startled yelp.

"What was that?" said a sailor's voice.

Kyro froze. He hadn't realized anyone had come down here. Sweat trickled down his back, and he spit the sour taste from his mouth, not daring to grab his canteen until the sailor went on his way.

"Who's there?" the voice called again. "If there's a stowaway down here, you'd best come out now and we might not throw you overboard."

Kyro shivered. *Please don't let him be serious.*

A creak echoed as the sailor pried open one of the other crates. Would he go through all of them? Should Kyro surrender or hope he might remain undiscovered?

His hesitation cost him. When the sailor found nothing in the first crate, he moved over to Kyro's, and before he knew what was happening, the sailor yanked him from the crate by his shirt collar in one hand and Cypher in the other.

"What have we here?" It was one of the sailors Kyro had encountered on the docks earlier in the day. Recognition crossed the man's face. "I remember you. You were the scamp trying to get free passage this morning."

He dropped the pair unceremoniously to the floor and loomed over Kyro. "I've got news for you, boy. The captain doesn't take kindly to stowaways. None of us do." The sailor shoved Cypher into Kyro's hands and then dragged him up the stairs to the main deck.

"I'm sorry, I didn't mean to—"

The sailor laughed. "What? Didn't mean to sneak into the crate and take a nap? I'm sure that's exactly what happened."

Fear slid over Kyro's skin and sank into his bones.

When they reached the main deck, the boat swayed hard and Kyro stumbled, but the sailor ensured he stayed upright. The ocean spread out as far as the eye could see in every direction, frothy and fuming and teeming with unseen life. Queasiness washed over him again.

The sailor carted him past several other scowling crew members, then straight up to a cabin at one end of the ship. He opened the door and pushed Kyro and Cypher inside.

Kyro guessed it was the captain's quarters. The room had several tables filled with maps and various seafaring instruments that he didn't recognize. Shelves of books and knick-knacks, many of which glinted with gold, lined the walls. Kyro nearly started when he caught sight of one thing he did recognize, tucked between two books: a pair of starglass goggles. Behind the desk at the center of the room sat a woman with wildly curly dark hair and a grim expression. Kyro gulped. He was beyond curious to know what she was doing with a rare item like starglass goggles, but was too afraid to ask.

"Captain Salban, I found this boy stowed away in a crate

belowdecks. He was asking about passage to Drenn this morning. Guess he didn't want to pay for a real room aboard *The Celestine*."

The woman stood and glared, towering over him. "You're dismissed, Sully," she said to the sailor, who ducked out of the room as quickly as he could, leaving Kyro to face the woman alone. He shrank back, and Cypher whined to be put down.

Captain Salban perched on the edge of her desk. "So, tell me, boy, what made you think you could stow away on my ship? It's quite rude. Don't they teach you manners where you come from?"

Kyro's free hand quivered at his side. "I—I'm sorry. I was desperate to get home to Drenn."

Captain Salban harrumphed. "Why? And why, pray tell, are you traveling alone?"

Kyro straightened up. "I'm not alone. I have my dog, Cypher, with me."

Salban laughed. "I was referring to human companions. Such as your parents."

Kyro stared down at his shoes. The ship lurched again, and he turned an uncomfortable shade of green.

"Never been on a ship before, have you, boy?" She opened a drawer in her desk and handed a small hard candy to Kyro. "This will help. It's bad enough that you stowed away. I can't have you making a mess of my cabin too."

"Thank you," he said, popping the candy in his mouth. It had an unusual spice to it, something like ginger.

"Come, sit." Salban gestured to a chair. "Tell me the whole story."

Kyro did as he was told, not daring to disobey the formidable woman. When his paws hit the floor, Cypher waltzed right up to Salban and wagged his tail like he was expecting a treat. Kyro held his breath. Salban considered the dog for a moment. Then a small smile cracked her lips, and she reached down to scratch Cypher behind the ears. Satisfied, the dog trotted back to his master and curled up under his chair.

"My father is a Star Shepherd, and our watchtower is near the village of Drenn. I crossed the Black Lands to get to Daluth. I didn't dare return that way."

Salban absorbed this information with hardly a blink. "You were there for the Star Shepherd Council meeting then. Bunch of old fools, the lot of them." She scoffed. "Where's your father now?"

Kyro bristled, but tried not to let it show. To be fair, her assessment of the Council wasn't wrong. "Yes, I was at the meeting. But my father was not. He was the reason for the meeting, actually. He went missing a week ago."

The captain raised an eyebrow. "You mean you crossed the Black Lands alone?"

Kyro shivered as he nodded.

"That's impressive for someone so young. And incredibly foolish. What happened to your father?"

Kyro paused. He wasn't sure he could trust the captain, but his gut told him that he shouldn't hold anything back. Not if he wanted to be on this ship when it reached Drenn.

"Something is wrong with the stars. When my father told the Council, they did nothing. He believes someone is stealing them, and he's searching for them. Now the Council has decided that he abandoned his post and has forbidden him—and me—from touching the stars ever again. I was at the meeting to plead my father's case."

Salban frowned. "You left your tower with no one to watch it?"

"A friend is watching in my absence." *At least I hope she is*, Kyro thought.

"Then I suppose I can't say you're irresponsible. Unlike your father."

Kyro's hands balled into fists in his lap. "He's not irresponsible. He's trying to save the stars."

"And yet he left you, a novice, behind to cover his sworn duties in the process."

Kyro couldn't help wondering who this woman was, and how she knew so much about Star Shepherding, but he got the sense that asking would get him into trouble.

"He had to leave. The Council wouldn't help; he had no other choice. He cares too much about the stars to sit back and watch them die."

The captain was quiet for a moment, and then her expression softened. "You're a good son. And a brave one too. It does you credit."

But before she could say anything else, an awful noise sounded from the deck. It was one Kyro knew well: the sound of gears crunching when something was caught in the works.

Captain Salban sprang up and strode onto the deck, with Kyro trailing after. Sailors raced to and fro, trying to get the ship's sails under control. Kyro could see from here that smoke coiled out from the rigging high up on the mast.

"What happened?" Salban grabbed the nearest crew member.

"Not sure, Captain. The sail just stopped working as we tried to turn toward Drenn."

"Well, fix it!"

"We're not sure how. It's brand new, and they're supposed to last for a decade," the sailor said.

Kyro tugged at Captain Salban's sleeve. "Excuse me," he said.

She frowned at him. "Not now. Go back to my cabin. I'll deal with you later."

Kyro took a deep breath. "But I can fix the rigging, ma'am. My father was a clockmaker before he became a Star Shepherd."

The captain's eyes roved back to Kyro. "You know how to fix this?"

His heart thundered against his ribs. *I sure hope so*, he thought.

"Yes. I've seen gears that work like that before. They're simple, really, and your sailor is right; they should last for years."

"Then why aren't they working?"

Kyro squinted up at the sails. "See those sticks? It looks like a bird made a nest in there. It's messing up the works and probably made a cog fall out of place." He scanned the deck, then found what he was searching for. "See, here it is." He picked up the glinting piece of brass that had gone unnoticed over by the edge of the ship.

Captain Salban considered Kyro for a moment longer. "All right, if you can fix that rigging, you might just earn yourself passage. Go on," she said.

Nervous energy filled Kyro's limbs as he was given a harness the sailors used to clamber up the mast to the crow's nest. He grabbed the small case of tools he had brought with him in his pack, and held his breath as one of the sailors helped him shinny up the mast.

Don't look down, don't look down, Kyro said to himself over and over. With the way the mast swayed, he was very, very glad that the captain had given him that ginger candy earlier.

When he reached the smoking part of the rigging, he set to work clearing out the empty nest. He was relieved to see that the design of the rigging was relatively simple—far simpler than his father's cart—and with the right tools and a careful touch, he should be able to make short work of it.

First, he gently adjusted the remaining gears that had been twisted out of place. Then he replaced the one that had fallen to the deck. He tightened a few more bolts and screws, then sighed with relief as the gears moved properly again.

"Lower me down!" he called. Descending was far worse, but he closed his eyes and climbed down the mast, not opening them until his feet hit the boards of the deck.

"Give it a whirl, First Mate," the captain ordered, and the sailor behind the steering wheel turned it toward Drenn and pressed the button controlling the sails. The clockwork in the rigging clicked, and the sails pivoted. A cheer went up from the crew.

Salban gave Kyro an appraising look. "As a general rule, I dislike Star Shepherds on principle. Your Council and your father are exactly why." She cracked her knuckles, making Kyro jump. "But I like you, boy. I'll let you stay on until Drenn. You've been through enough, and we're halfway there anyway. What's your name?"

Kyro's eyes were wide. "My name is Kyro."

"Well, Kyro of Drenn," Salban clasped his hand in her leathery grip. "Welcome to *The Celestine*."

CHAPTER SEVENTEEN

THE CAPTAIN INTRODUCED KYRO TO THE FIRST MATE, Sully—the same man who had found him in the cargo hold—properly this time. The man shook Kyro's hand and smiled, showing a few blackened teeth.

"Well done, boy."

"We'll reach Drenn in a couple hours, just before dawn," Captain Salban said. "Until then, you can tell me more about what's plaguing the stars."

"Yes, ma'am," Kyro said.

"I prefer Salban."

Whether Kyro liked it or not, he was going to have to trust

her with more of his secrets. It was a fair price. He didn't want to find out what would happen if the captain changed her mind about letting him remain aboard *The Celestine*.

She brought Kyro to the railing of the ship where they could see the stars bobbing over the horizon. The boat rocked, and the sea churned beneath them. Cypher barked and chased the gulls around the deck while the captain looked on, amused, as she leaned against the railing.

"Now, tell me, what was so urgent that your father had to leave? What made him think someone's taking the stars?" She glanced at the sky, and Kyro couldn't help thinking that she seemed nervous.

"One night we noticed that a star's burlap case had been sliced open. Usually when they fall off the hooks, they leave a jagged tear." Kyro's heart chilled at the memory. "It was like someone had cut it down instead."

Salban's brow furrowed. "No one alive can reach the stars. Unless you catapulted them up there, but the ride down would be a death sentence."

"Exactly. My father reported it to the Council immediately, but they thought nothing of it. And when he got home, he told me that other Star Shepherds had reported seeing dark shadow creatures called the vissla."

She stood up straight. "What?"

"They're shadow creatures, and—"

"Yes, yes, I know what the vissla are. There've been sightings of them? They're returning?" Alarm filled her face.

"I've seen them myself."

She stepped closer. "You're serious? What was it like?"

Kyro gazed out at the waves lapping the sides of the ship and swallowed hard. "It was cold, like it radiated pure evil. One of them got to a star before me, and the vissla killed it."

Salban leaned back on her elbows. "And those fools at the Council ignored that?" She scowled. "Idiots. So certain nothing will change that by the time they realize they're wrong, it'll be far too late."

"That's not all," Kyro said. "My father only took off after two clusters of stars fell in one night. We couldn't go after the first. It was far away in the Radamak Mountains, but the second was right in our woods. When we reached them, all that remained were smoking craters. Someone had stolen every single star. We couldn't rescue any of them." His eyes burned at the memory.

Salban gasped. "You told this to the Council too?"

"Of course. I had to justify why my father left." Kyro decided to leave out the fact that his father had cried wolf to the Council a few too many times, which was why they hadn't taken his father's or his own claims seriously.

"And they still did nothing?"

"They did *something*," Kyro said. "They banned me and my

father from saving the stars." A bitter taste formed in the back of his throat.

"Then they've grown stupider with age."

A thought nagged at Kyro. "How do you know so much about the Council and Star Shepherds? No one else I've met has had a clue what the vissla are."

Salban's eyes glinted. "It's time for me to tell *you* a story now."

She told him tale after tale he had never heard before. He doubted even his father knew them. Kyro examined Salban while Cypher snoozed in his lap. She appeared to be merely a ship's captain, but she was very knowledgeable about the stars. Her connection to them had to be far more personal than she was willing to let on. He wished his father could meet her.

"How do you know all these stories?" Kyro asked. He'd been trying to hold his curiosity inside, but he was ready to burst. "Were you a Star Shepherd once?"

Salban laughed. "Not exactly. But you could say it's in my blood. I come from a long line of them. These stories were passed down through my family."

Kyro frowned. "Why are you so hard on the Council then?"

Salban's face grew more serious. "Not all Star Shepherds favor the Council, and as you've seen for yourself, the Council doesn't favor all Star Shepherds either. You could say my family had something of a falling-out with them long ago." She straightened up, with a new glint in her eyes. "Now, have you heard the one about the descendants of the Seven Elders?" Salban asked.

"No, I don't know it."

"When the Elders sent their hearts into the sky, their fame lasted only for a few hundred years. People became accustomed to safety and forgot all about the dangers of the dark creatures the stars held back. The world's belief in their power dwindled, and the legend of the Seven Elders was relegated to bedtime stories and campfires.

"But the descendants of the Seven Elders carried the flame of knowledge as best they could in the face of the world's lack of faith. Until even some of the descendants' children began to doubt. The descendants knew they couldn't let the knowledge of the stars die out. They had to do something. They devised a way to prolong their lives by splicing a piece of their own hearts with a star. As long as the star remained hanging in the skies, that descendant would continue to live on."

Kyro's mouth dropped open. "Those stars must have all fallen by now, haven't they?"

Salban shrugged. "I'd expect so, but who knows? There are thousands of stars. Eventually they formed the Star Shepherd Council to ensure the secrets of the stars were passed down from generation to generation, and that their protection would be of paramount importance."

Kyro scratched his head. "Well, what happened to—"

"Land ho!" cried a sailor on the other side of the ship. Kyro stood up from the railing.

The village of Drenn could be seen by starlight, getting closer every second. Kyro frowned. Something looked odd about the port. He ran to the other side of the bow and leaned out over the railing to see better. Sea spray spattered his chin.

"What is it?" Salban sauntered over. Cypher whined at Kyro's side.

Kyro squinted. Something was obscuring his vision of the port, and he couldn't quite figure out—

"It's smoking. The port is smoking." he said.

Salban sat up immediately. "Sully! Fire up the engines right now!" Her command was met with a few concerned looks, but no hesitation. The boat began to move through the water at a faster pace. Kyro's heart had frozen. He hoped against hope that what he thought might be happening was not the case.

The boat finally reached a spot where they had a full view of the port, straight up the hill to the market square.

The cause of the smoke was suddenly all too clear.

Something had set all of Drenn ablaze.

CHAPTER EIGHTEEN

KYRO STOOD FROZEN AT THE RAILING, TRANSFIXED BY the sight before him. He couldn't even utter the cry strangled in his chest. The center of the town glowed like a beacon, with flames of yellow and orange shooting up here and there. Smoke billowed over the docks like a dark cloud creeping across the water toward them.

"Here," Captain Salban said, startling Kyro back to life. She held a bandanna out to him and then tied her own over her nose. "You don't want to breathe that in." She called over her shoulder to the crew. "Hurry up and ready the rowboat. We can't dock here yet, or we risk going up in flames too."

"But what about—" Kyro began.

"Don't worry." Salban put a firm hand on his shoulder. "I'll get you home and see what we can salvage."

She pushed him toward the side of the ship, Cypher close at their heels, and helped him clamber into the rowboat. Two other sailors joined them with supplies and buckets, and took up the remaining oars. Unlike the steamship, the rowboat was not fitted with clockwork upgrades to help it move faster. But the crew took *The Celestine* as close as they could to the shore before Salban shouted to Sully to lower them to the water. The rowboat jerked and halted on its way down, making Kyro's stomach flip. Cypher whined, and Kyro wrapped his arms around him, burying his face in the dog's fur.

Then they hit the water, and the sailors rowed, the boat gliding through the waves and the thick smoke. Kyro's eyes burned, and he was grateful for Salban's quick thinking with the bandanna. The trip would have been a hundred times worse without it.

It was hard to see, but the sailors knew their route well. The boat bumped against the dock much faster than Kyro had dared to hope. Salban helped him out of the boat, and he set Cypher on the dock beside him. "Stay close," he whispered to his dog.

The fire was focused mainly in the market area. Villagers ran to and fro, desperately trying to extinguish the buildings that had been set alight.

Andra.

Kyro's feet had begun to move, when Salban pulled him back.

"Where do you think you're going without a bucket? Do you expect to put out the fire just by telling it to behave?" The captain shoved a bucket into his hands. "Here, fill this up."

The other sailors were dipping their buckets in the ocean, then heaving them up. Kyro followed suit and soon trailed the others as they rushed into the marketplace. Chaos reigned, along with light and heat and smoke. It was disorienting. Kyro might very well have gotten lost if not for Salban once again pointing him in the right direction.

"See that building over there?" She gestured to the butcher's shop. "Let's work on that first. It's on the edges of the fire. We have to beat this back."

Kyro could hear the fire hissing on the other side of the square as water from a hose hit the flames. He and the sailors ran back and forth to the dock several times, quenching as many buildings on the fringes as they could. The fire finally sputtered out, meeting its end from the suffocating hose.

The first rays of dawn spread across the sky, erasing the stars from view. Kyro had seen the dawn many, many times of course, but this time it felt different. Like he wasn't sure how many of those stars would remain when night fell again.

Behind them on the docks, *The Celestine* was moored,

groaning and creaking and drawing attention. When the villagers saw Kyro, murmurs and scowls filled the crowd. A familiar figure burst through the ranks, hurling himself at Kyro before he had a chance to react.

Bodin, red-faced and livid, yanked Kyro off the ground by the collar of his shirt. Cypher barked and tugged at the hem of Kyro's pants, but Bodin didn't seem to notice.

"You!" Bodin sputtered. "This is all your fault! This is your doing! You and your father's treachery. We've lost four shops, burned to ash, and it's all thanks to you."

Kyro's mouth hung slack in shock as Bodin shook him. "Well, what do you have to say for yourself, boy?"

"Leave him alone!" Andra—who Kyro hadn't even noticed approaching—shoved her father from behind. "He wasn't even here. He had nothing to do with the fire."

"Get back, Andra," Bodin growled. "Or you'll be grounded for the rest of your days. I've had enough of your infatuation with this fool boy."

Andra's face turned beet red. "I will do no such thing. You put him down right now, or I'll never talk to you again!"

"I swear, sir, I had nothing to do with the fire. I was on a ship. We were just trying to help when we got here."

Bodin shook Kyro again for good measure. "Stop lying. You know this is all on your and your father's heads."

To Kyro's great surprise, Captain Salban laid a hand on

Bodin's arm. "Bodin," she said quietly. "It's been a long time, hasn't it? Why don't you put the boy down? I can vouch for him. He was with me all night, and we were together when we saw the fire from the bow of my ship. Whatever you think he did, it wasn't him."

Bodin's face shifted from rage to shock, and then, most surprising of all, to sheepish acceptance. He set Kyro's feet back on the ground and released his shirt. Andra ran over to Kyro and hugged him fiercely; he hugged her back in a daze.

"Salban?" Bodin said. "It's really you?"

"In the flesh. Though I didn't expect to find you bullying a mere boy." She put her hands on her hips, and Bodin took a step back under her gaze. Behind him, the murmurs in the crowd began to transform to angry grumbles.

"Things have changed. Ever since that boy"—he pointed at Kyro—"and his father came to Drenn, they have caused nothing but mischief. And tonight they nearly destroyed our livelihood."

"A Star Shepherd and his son? What could they possibly have done?"

"Nothing!" Andra cried, clenching her fists. "Nothing at all."

But the swelling crowd did not seem to agree with Andra. Something hot and urgent formed in Kyro's gut as they began to yell.

"It's him! He did it!" cried a villager.

"He brought the sky down on our heads!" yelled another.

Salban shook her head. "What on earth happened here, Bodin? Explain yourself right now."

"It was the stars. That's why we believe *he* had something to do with the fire."

Kyro frowned, puzzled. "What do you mean?"

Bodin turned his eyes to him as if he had forgotten Kyro was even there. "A whole slew of them crashed right here in the market. Set the rooftops ablaze. We're lucky no one was killed."

The villagers' cries grew louder, and the crowd steadily inched closer. Kyro couldn't help drawing back and bumped into Salban. Then another familiar face pushed his way to the front of the crowd and stood at Kyro's side. This time it was one Kyro was relieved to see: Doman, possibly the only person in Drenn who actually liked his father.

"Bodin, you fool. Star Shepherds don't control the stars; they just rescue them," Doman said.

Salban barked a laugh. "Is *that* what they all believe?" She glared at the crowd. "Kyro and his father haven't a clue when a star will fall. If they did, do you think they'd actually stay up all night every night just to watch the skies for fun?" She scoffed. "And now you've got them whipped into a frenzy about it."

"Kyro, we need to leave," Doman said as the crowd began to move closer.

But the second Kyro turned toward the docks, the crowd roared and the villagers lurched toward him.

"Don't let him get away!"

"Someone has to pay for this destruction!"

Cold fear froze Kyro to the bone.

"Oh, come on, you big fool," Salban admonished Bodin. "Help us get him out of here. There's a riot about to break out, thanks to you."

Bodin's face turned red, but his expression was one Kyro hadn't seen on him before: regret.

Doman grabbed Kyro by the arm, bringing him back to his senses, while Bodin, cowed by Salban, hurried them down an alleyway as villagers poured after them. Andra sprinted ahead of her father, anticipating where he was taking them. They wound through alleys until Kyro was dizzy. Then finally they found themselves on a street that was quiet and empty—for now. The shouts of the villagers were not very far behind.

"We should go to my house," Doman said. "It's nearby."

"Why?" Kyro asked.

Doman paused as the eyes of Salban and her sailors appraised him. "Because I have information there about your father."

CHAPTER NINETEEN

KYRO YANKED HIS ARM OUT OF DOMAN'S GRASP. "WHAT are you talking about?"

The large man shifted from foot to foot. "Come with me. I'll explain everything."

Captain Salban rolled her eyes, but nudged Kyro toward Doman. "Go," she said. "We'll keep the villagers away. Get to safety."

With a last look back at the others, especially Andra, Kyro set off with Doman, following him down the alley toward his cottage on the edge of the village. Before long, the cottage and its metal roof came into view. Doman held the door open, checking to be sure they weren't followed by any of the other villagers. Kyro ducked inside with Cypher at his heels.

The inside of the cottage was filled with ironwork in much the same way Kyro's home was filled with clockwork. There was a metal table with wrought-iron legs and crafted chairs next to it, and metal sconces illuminated the room. Doman offered one of the chairs, but a frenetic energy now possessed Kyro. Doman had information about his father. Sitting was impossible.

"Wait here," Doman said as he hurried into a back room. When he returned, he was carrying a rucksack. Kyro eyed it curiously.

"Well?" Kyro said. "What do you know about what happened to my father?"

Doman sank into one of the metal chairs, rubbing his hands over his craggy face. "I'm sorry, Kyro. I lied when you came to my shop and asked if I'd seen Tirin. He explicitly instructed me not to tell you anything."

Kyro's knees turned to rubber. He sat quietly on a chair, his face twisting. What had he done to make his father mistrust him so? He'd tried to be a good son; he'd done everything Tirin asked of him. He'd sat by and watched as his father spiraled deeper and deeper into his obsession and farther and farther away from his son's reach.

None of it mattered. Not to his father. All that mattered was whatever mission he got into his head that he needed to fulfill.

Kyro didn't realize his fingers had clenched into fists until Doman's large hand cupped his shoulder. "Don't blame him too harshly, Kyro. In his mind, he did it to protect you."

"Protect me?" Kyro sputtered. "From what? The vissla have returned, the sky is falling, and someone is stealing the stars. If he really wanted to protect me, he would be *here*."

"I don't disagree. But he was very insistent when he left. I figured it was just another of his larks. Some silly idea he'd gotten into his head and that he'd be back in a day or two." Doman let out a breath. "But Tirin has been gone much too long. It isn't like him to leave his tower unmanned. The stars mean everything to him. I fear something is wrong. Someone needs to go after him."

A chill made its way down Kyro's spine. Doman's words hit on his secret fear, the creeping thought that had been prickling at the back of his brain every day since his father disappeared.

Only something terrible could keep him away from his duties for this long.

"What can I do?" Kyro asked as raw, biting helplessness spread through his gut.

"We'll go after him. He told me he was planning to return to the village of Romvi. We should start there. And," Doman held out the rucksack to Kyro, "he left this in my care. I haven't opened it. But I think you should have it."

Kyro took the rucksack, equal parts curious and furious.

It was as though his father had abandoned him all over again, leaving nothing but questions behind. Cypher nuzzled against his knee, and Kyro absentmindedly scratched his dog's head.

But before they could discuss the best route to Romvi, echoes from the streets beyond Doman's door startled them. It was the unmistakable sound of an angry mob. Kyro tensed in his chair.

Doman leapt to his feet. "Go, Kyro. And grab what you can from the pantry on your way out. Quickly now, out the back. I'll catch up to you when I can."

Kyro obeyed without question and fled out the back door, Cypher matching him step for step. At first he wasn't sure what direction to go, but he decided on north, and ran as fast as his legs would carry him.

When the mob reached Doman's cottage, Kyro wanted to be as far away as possible.

But as he approached the village gates, a new sound reached his ears. One small voice, growing louder by the second.

"Starboy! Wait!"

Kyro turned in amazement. There was Andra running after him, arms waving.

"What are you doing here?" Kyro asked when she stopped at his side.

She wrinkled her nose at him, only slightly out of breath. "I'm going with you, of course. Doman told me you're headed to Romvi. He's still busy keeping the villagers occupied. You're not going alone."

"Andra, you've already gotten in enough trouble because of me." Kyro desperately didn't want to go on this journey alone, but he couldn't help feeling somewhat responsible for Andra's recent spats with her father.

"No, Kyro. I got into trouble because I chose to help a friend. And I choose the same now."

"But your father—"

"My father is a fool. And really, I think he's frightened of you." She pushed loose strands of dark hair behind her ears. "I'm not scared. And I'm ready to help. This is my choice, not yours."

Startled by the force of Andra's conviction, Kyro smiled gratefully. He really didn't want to be alone, not for this. Not anymore.

"Thank you," he said. "We should get going then?"

"Definitely. And as fast as possible." Together, they ran through the gates, Cypher dodging between them, and disappeared into the forest.

CHAPTER TWENTY

AS THEY HURRIED THROUGH THE FOREST, KYRO CON-
sulted the map he still had in his pack. There were two ways
to reach Romvi. They could cut through the Ergsada Valley
Desert, or they could travel the steep hills that edged it. The
hills were technically the shorter path, but it would take
them much longer to cross. The desert looked like it would
be their best bet. Thankfully, the Ergsada Valley, while still
dangerous, wasn't anywhere near as bleak or treacherous as
the Black Lands.

Kyro sighed. If only Romvi were a port town, maybe
Captain Salban could have given them a ride there and made

the journey faster. As it was, they should reach Romvi by late afternoon, if they were lucky. But only if they didn't stop to rest.

Kyro explained the options to Andra, and they decided to press on for the desert without stopping at Kyro's watchtower to pick up more supplies. Andra had brought a little money (which apparently Salban had guilted her father into giving her), so they could buy food. They'd split the remaining supplies already in Kyro's pack on the way.

Ever since Doman had told Kyro his father was headed to Romvi, an odd feeling had begun to well up inside him. Kyro had loved Romvi. It was where he and his family had been happy. Back when his mother was still alive. Life had been filled with friends, family, and laughter. In Drenn, all of those things were in short supply. Returning to Romvi only reminded Kyro of what he'd lost. He couldn't imagine what would take his father there now.

"How does your father know the captain?" Kyro asked. The more he learned about Salban, the more his curiosity grew. Her connections to the Star Shepherds had made her all the more intriguing.

"She said something about hanging out on the docks when they were kids, so they must have known each other growing up. My dad did want to be a sailor for a time before he decided to take over his parents' bakery." Andra shrugged. "Who knows? I'm just glad it worked in my favor." She grinned, and Kyro laughed.

It wasn't long before the forest thinned, the ground beneath their feet turned grainy and dry, and the plants grew sparser and farther apart. Soon, the yellow sands of the Ergsada Valley were churning in front of them in great sloping waves. Unlike the Black Lands, there were no skeletal remains of long-lost structures clawing out from the ground here. It was smooth, rolling sand as far as the eye could see. It almost looked like no one had ever disturbed the dunes before. Kyro shivered. The Black Lands had been disconcerting, but this seemed so vast, like it might swallow them whole.

Kyro and Cypher paused before the sands, and Andra wrinkled her nose at them. "Are you all right?"

Kyro tried to laugh, but it came out more like a groan. "I was just thinking that I've already had my fill of deserts this week." He shrugged. "But there's no help for it."

And with that, they set out into the yawning expanse before them.

Andra spoke first. "How did the Council meeting go? Did they agree to let your father remain a Star Shepherd?"

Kyro's shoulders slumped. Amid all the excitement, he had almost forgotten about the Council's terrible verdict. "No, they didn't."

"But why not?" Andra kicked at a crest of sand, spraying the fine stuff in front of her.

"I couldn't defend his actions to their satisfaction. And not enough of them believed what I had to say about the stars being cut down. Both of us are now banned from touching the stars."

Andra placed a hand on Kyro's shoulder and squeezed. "What an awful thing to do. You were just trying to make things right, after all. It isn't fair for them to punish you for it."

Kyro picked up a wayward pebble, rubbing the smooth stone between his thumb and forefinger, then tossed it at the horizon. It skipped over the sand as if it were water. "I wish they hadn't. But there was nothing I could say to change their minds. They'd decided before I got there."

Andra's hands balled into fists at her sides. "Well, that's just not right. I'd tell them that, if they were here."

Kyro gave his friend a half-hearted smile. "Thanks."

The sun rose higher, and the day grew hotter and drier. Soon they were sweltering as they trudged through the sands. They were about halfway to Romvi when Cypher—who had been running ahead—yapped. Kyro's heart leapt, and he broke into a run.

He hadn't forgotten the last time Cypher had run off in a desert. He'd almost lost him.

When he reached his dog, Kyro was relieved to see Cypher wasn't in trouble. But he had certainly found…something.

Andra caught up to him and stopped short. "What on earth is that?"

Cypher pawed at something sticking out from the sand. They knelt down to examine it.

"It looks like some kind of metal canister," Kyro said, shaking his head. "But I couldn't tell you what it was for."

"Or why it looks like someone tore it in half," Andra said, eyeing the jagged edges.

Cypher began to dig more determinedly around it, and Kyro and Andra helped to free the metal object. But the deeper they dug, the clearer it became that this wasn't a mere canister. There was a bend farther down. It was hard work, but their curiosity was at the boiling point; they had to know what this was. Finally, they removed enough sand to yank the huge object free. They stumbled back, nearly dropping their prize.

This was definitely not a canister.

It was a gigantic mechanical arm—taller than Kyro—ripped off whatever body it had once belonged to, with an elbow joint and a forearm that ended in grasping metal fingers.

Kyro's heart pounded in his ears. He couldn't help remembering his mother's stories about the metal giants. This arm was big enough to belong to one of them.

"How is this possible?" Andra asked, astonished.

"I don't know..." Kyro said. "It reminds me of the story of the giants. But they've been gone for centuries."

Andra touched the arm with awe. "Maybe this is one of the ancient ones. Maybe it fell out here in the dunes centuries ago, and we just found it now." She swept her arm at the desert surrounding them. "Who knows what else might be buried out here?"

As she spoke, something else glinted in the sun and caught Kyro's eye. He left the mechanical arm on the sand and ran toward the glimmering object. When he reached it, his heart took a seat in his throat.

It was unmistakable, a thing he would recognize anywhere: a star hook, severed in a clean cut. Just like the ones he and Andra had found not long ago. Andra gasped behind him, then shouted. "Look! There's another one!"

Sure enough, another severed hook rested nearby. They found several more in the area, but try as they might, not a single burlap casing or star heart was anywhere to be found. It was as though someone had taken them and left only the hooks behind. And perhaps that arm. Though that last bit seemed too impossible to imagine.

"What do you think happened here?" Andra asked.

Kyro shivered. "I don't know. But if it has anything to do with the stars, it might be related to my father's disappearance."

Andra grew serious and tucked the star hook she was holding into her bag. "Then we best get going and find out."

CHAPTER TWENTY-ONE

THE SUN WAS SETTLING BEHIND THE RADAMAK Mountains when they reached Romvi. The sight of the village's familiar thatched roofs surrounding the tall spire of a watchtower in the very center—the one his grandparents had manned before he was born—made Kyro's breath hitch in his throat.

Kyro frowned and rubbed the back of his head. The best memories he had were made here. Seeing it now was a painful reminder of how much he missed his old life and the time when he had both his mother and father.

While Drenn was surrounded by a forest on one side and a bay on the other, Romvi was flanked by acres of rolling fields filled with grains and vegetables, the Radamak Mountains looming in the distance behind. There was less bustle here; the atmosphere was more relaxed and friendly. And they didn't mind Star Shepherds. At least, that was how it used to be.

"Is it at all like you remember?" Andra whispered, startling Kyro. Cypher whined by his side.

Kyro nodded. "Yes. At least, I think it is. I hope so."

"Should we ask the local Star Shepherd if they've seen your father?"

Kyro gritted his teeth. "Definitely not. I don't think he'd seek their help after the Council didn't believe his report. I don't know who is in charge of this territory now, but since most of the Council voted against him, whoever it is probably did too." He sighed. "They won't help us. They might even try to make us leave before we figure out what happened to my father."

After his grandparents passed away, the Romvi watchtower had remained vacant for some time before the Council filled the position. But his mother had often taken him there to show him where she had grown up and tell him stories about the stars. A new Shepherd had been assigned not long before she fell ill, so Kyro had never really known him. If only they hadn't filled the position, his father could have taken it over and they could have stayed in Romvi.

Kyro wondered if any of the people they had known still lived here. He'd had friends when he was little, but he doubted they'd remember him now. And he wasn't in the mood to explain what he was doing here if he could avoid it.

"I think it's best if we find my old house and see if that's where my father went," Kyro said.

Andra wrinkled her nose. "But what if someone else lives there now?"

Kyro's heart sunk into his shoes. He hadn't considered that, and he doubted his father had either. Hopefully, he hadn't caused too much trouble in this town too.

"Then we'll just have to explain why we're here, as much I don't want to. What choice do we have? This is our only lead. Maybe someone has at least seen my father, if nothing else."

A thought occurred to Kyro, and he pulled out the rucksack his father had left with Doman. "Actually, maybe it isn't our only lead…"

He and Andra rested under a willow tree at the edge of the village, while Cypher chased the fireflies that sparked in the dusk. Kyro placed the rucksack between them.

"My father left this in Doman's care, and Doman gave it to me. I was in such a hurry to leave Drenn that I nearly forgot about it."

"You mean, you haven't even opened it yet?" Andra said, eyes wide.

Kyro shook his head and put his hand inside. The first thing his fingers touched was something familiar, and he pulled it out eagerly, his face brightening with hope. The starglass goggles glinted at their sisters and brothers peeking out from the night sky above.

"Where did he get these?" Kyro murmured at the same time Andra said, "Don't you have some just like that?"

"I did," Kyro said. "Until the Council took them away when they forbade me and my father from ever touching the stars again." This was a jolting reminder of just how much he missed chasing the stars.

The goggles were perfect, not even a little bit dinged or dented. His father must have been hoarding an extra pair. Kyro carefully placed them around his neck, the familiar weight oddly comforting.

Andra squinted at the rucksack. "Anything else in there?"

Kyro fished around again, and his hand alighted on a glass container. When he opened his hand, a vial of stardust glinted up at him. That tiny glimmer in his heart warmed further. The goggles would help him find the stars, and the stardust could be used for protection against creatures like the vissla.

Maybe hope wasn't lost after all.

Andra laughed. "That's stardust, isn't it?"

Kyro nodded. "It has protective properties. My father must have been saving the stardust from stars he wasn't able to rescue before dawn for the last few years. It's what I used to keep the vissla from getting into our yard near the watchtower."

Andra nodded approvingly. "I remember. Good thing to have around."

Kyro agreed. But why had his father left these things with Doman? Why not give them to Kyro himself? He would have looked after them just fine. Or perhaps his father guessed what the Council would do and feared they would take the items from Kyro. Whatever the reason, they were his now, and he was glad of it.

Kyro stood and offered his hand to help Andra to her feet. Cypher yapped, as eager as they were to get to their destination. With a deep breath, Kyro stepped into the village, grateful that Andra had not let go of his hand. Hers was a steadying presence. And she made him bolder. Perhaps he should've let her come with him to the Star Shepherd Council meeting. Maybe she would've found a way to change the Council members' minds.

But what was done was done, and all that was left for Kyro was to find his father.

He led Andra and Cypher through the grid of streets in Romvi. He hadn't been here in years, but his feet remembered the way. The days when he ran through these streets and alleys with his friends had been the happiest time of his life. When his family was whole, not broken into shards like it was now.

On the way through the village, Andra ducked into a shop to quickly restock their supplies with the money her father had given her. After that, it didn't take long to reach the little house adjoining an old boarded-up shop front. A lump formed in Kyro's throat, and he wiped his clammy hands on his pants. Once, that had been his father's clockmaker's shop. It looked like no one had touched it since the day they left. To his relief, no one seemed to have moved into the house either. When he knocked, no one answered and the door was not locked, which he found surprising. He took a deep breath and pushed the door open, sending a puff of dust into the air like smoke.

He and Andra both sneezed, while Cypher trotted inside, leaving paw prints on the dusty floor. They looked like they were dancing with a recent set of boot prints, illuminated by the starlight slipping in through the windows and open door.

Kyro went still as a statue. Those boot prints could easily belong to his father.

"He was here," Kyro whispered, pausing in the doorway. A small part of him was almost afraid to disturb the ghosts of his past who might linger in this house. As though stepping through would destroy the happy memories he once had like fragile glass bubbles.

Andra waited for Kyro to make a move, but he remained frozen on the threshold of the house. She nudged him.

"Do you think your father is still around?"

That shook Kyro out of his funk. "Let's find out." He stepped inside, stirring up more dust. He couldn't help hoping his father was here, hidden away somewhere upstairs, sleeping. Then Kyro's search would be over, and his father could fix things for real. Then they could go home.

But as they moved through the house, Cypher yapping and sniffing everything in sight, they found only shadows and empty corners. Enough dust was disturbed to make it clear his father had been here recently, but he was gone. The house was abandoned yet again.

Hollowness expanded under Kyro's ribs, filling him up until it threatened to make him burst. It seemed his father was always leaving. Kyro angrily kicked the leg of a table, sending up yet another puff of dust. The cloth covering the table slipped, revealing a pile of papers underneath. Kyro realized the cloth was not nearly as dusty as everything else.

"Andra!" he cried. "Over here."

She reached his side as he yanked the cloth away. A mess of notes and maps and star charts were strewn over the table.

"Looks like he definitely was here," Andra said, picking up one of the maps and wrinkling her brow. "And he was busy. There are notes all over this."

Kyro took one of the other maps of the region and examined it. Most of the notes made no sense to him, but one thing was clear from the path charted on the map. His father had been planning a journey—directly into the darkest, tallest peak of the Radamak Mountains.

Cold whispered down Kyro's spine. Though most people were no longer superstitious when it came to the stars, they were when it came to the mountains. The Radamak Mountains were rumored to be filled with wild beasts and dark things. Whatever his father's reason for going there, it wasn't good.

And Kyro was going to have to follow him.

"You don't think your father really went into the mountains, do you?" she said. Even fearless Andra had a slight tremor in her voice at the thought of braving the Radamaks.

Kyro could only nod, his throat too dry to respond properly. Cypher whined and settled at his feet, resting his head on crossed paws.

Kyro shuffled through his father's notes, hoping to find more clues of why he had decided to venture into the mountains. Only the other day, his father had explained how they were forbidden from going there! And now here he was, doing exactly that. Something significant must have changed his mind, and Kyro suspected it had to be something more than just the lost stars.

There had to be something else here that explained it.

He and Andra scanned the notes, looking for more than his father's ravings. The first few Kyro read held no surprises—all talk of the desecrated stars and the vissla's return. But then a small sheet of paper tucked beneath several maps revealed a story. His father, it seemed, had been interviewing people who lived near the Radamak Mountains. Over the last few years, there had been rumors of rare sightings of strange mechanical giants. Huge creatures—some that could even fly.

Kyro had to sit down, his hands trembling and shaking the paper. Andra looked at him. "What did you find?"

"Remember that mechanical arm we found in the desert?"

She grinned. "Of course. That was wonderful."

"It's real. And recent. A giant, alive now, today. My father has been collecting reports of sightings of the mechanical giants." He glanced back down at the report and shuddered. "And the rumors say they live in the Radamak Mountains. If we hadn't found that arm in the desert, I'd think he's mad, but…"

"But it's too much of a coincidence not to be true, isn't it?" Andra said, finishing Kyro's thought.

"Exactly. He must think they can help somehow. Put a stop to the vissla or whoever is taking the stars. We have to go after him." Kyro leapt to his feet, but Andra put a hand on his arm.

"You're exhausted. We all are," she said, gesturing to Cypher, already snoring under the table. "We need to sleep first, then we can head out in the morning."

Kyro hated waiting, but he couldn't deny that sleep would be welcome. Every part of his body ached from the long trek across the desert.

"All right," he said. He showed her where his parents' old bedroom was, and was glad to see it wasn't too dusty once he took the sheeting off the bed. He surveyed the room, a heavy thickness settling into his chest. Visions of his mother, pale and sickly, flitted through his mind like taunting ghosts. His heart raced as he left the room in a hurry.

Then he found himself in the bedroom of his childhood, just the same as the day they left it, covered in a thick sheen of dust. A smattering of old clockwork toys his father had crafted for him dotted the bedside table, almost as though they'd been waiting for him to return. Nothing had changed here, but everything had changed for him. He took the covering off his bed too and climbed in, trying to sleep as best he could. Bittersweet memories settled over him like a blanket of ice. Cypher had woken when they left the kitchen, and now he jumped up to settle in by his master's feet. Kyro was grateful for the little bit of warmth and companionship.

He lay awake for a long time, his heart pounding against his ribs. When he was little and his mother had told him the stories about the stars, he had thought how wondrous it would be to see the mechanical giants in real life. But he had long written that idea off as a foolish childhood fantasy. Now, to discover they may actually still exist was both incredible and terrifying. What would they be like after so many centuries without their human creators? Were they just machines, or did they think like humans?

More importantly, would they be willing to help?

CHAPTER TWENTY-TWO

THEY SET OUT AT DAWN THE NEXT DAY, KYRO HOPING TO avoid any of the townspeople who might remember his father or recognize him. There were too many questions that he couldn't answer yet.

His father had dragged Kyro away from Romvi once before, and now he was forcing him away again. Recovering that sort of life—one filled with light and life and laughter—seemed impossible.

After the years in Drenn, Kyro had almost forgotten how superstitious the people of Romvi were about living in the shadows of the Radamak Mountains. If his father's notes were any indication, that superstition had grown worse over the last few years. When Kyro stepped out of his old house in the early morning light, he glanced up at the peaks, now clearly visible. They were dark and hulking, and the great spire—the most formidable of all the peaks in the range—rose above them all like a looming beast just waiting for the right moment to pounce.

Sweat broke out on Kyro's brow despite the cool air, but when Andra came up beside him and put her warm hand in his, he felt a little braver.

"Ready, Starboy?" she said. Kyro nodded, and with Cypher prancing in front of them, they set out on the path to the edge of the village. At first, it seemed to be easy going, but before long, the village around them began to wake up. They rounded a bend and almost ran into a milkman setting up his cart for his daily rounds. Kyro grabbed Andra and ducked back into the shadows of a nearby building. At first, Cypher didn't realize his master had stopped and only turned back when Kyro hissed at him to heel.

The milkman had been on this route since long before Kyro was born and might actually remember him. Andra gave Kyro a bemused look but didn't object to hiding in the shadows until the man finally went on his way. As soon as he was out of sight, Kyro breathed a sigh of relief.

"You know him?" Andra said.

Kyro nodded. "And I'd rather not have to explain my father's strange reappearance here."

They escaped without further incident and soon reached the foothills of the Radamak Mountains. The spire seemed even more magnificent the closer they got, and the terrain was rocky and dotted with spindly, grasping trees as they approached. One lone, narrow path wound through the mountains, making its way up to the top of the spire. There were no noises here. No birdsong, no telltale rustling of critters. A low hum, perhaps made by some insects, was all they heard. Even Cypher was strangely quiet. It felt as though the mountains themselves held their breath, waiting for Kyro and Andra to enter their trap.

But they had no other path to follow, no other hope of finding Tirin and the mystery he'd been chasing.

The only way out of their predicament was through.

"It's all uphill from here," Andra said with a nervous laugh. She was usually unflappable, so her nervousness made Kyro worry all the more. He couldn't shake the feeling of eyes crawling over them as they worked up enough courage to step onto the path and venture into the thick of the trees.

Within minutes, the canopy closed around them, blocking out the sun. When Kyro risked a glance back, he could no longer see Romvi—just trees and winding path. That was all there was before and behind them. Some of the trees had black smudges on their trunks, almost like scorch marks that only made the scenery more foreboding.

"Do you really think your father is lost in these woods?" Andra rubbed her arms.

Kyro shrugged. "Part of me hopes he is because it means we're on the right track, and the rest of me hopes he's not."

She laughed. "I can't blame you for that. Though I hope he is, so that this trek isn't for nothing." Her tone softened. "And so you can have him back."

Kyro tried to smile, but it felt wrong here in the Radamaks where everything was eternally drenched in twilight.

A few minutes later, Andra spoke again. "What if... What if we find him, and he doesn't want to come home?"

Kyro's hands shook. She had named the very question that haunted his own heart. "I don't know. If he still has more work to do to find the culprit taking the stars, then we can help him, I suppose." He kicked a wayward stick. "If he'll let us, of course. If not, then I'll just have to do my best to convince him he's needed in Drenn to save the stars there."

Andra put a hand on Kyro's shoulder. "*We* will convince him."

"Thanks," Kyro said.

They trudged on in silence. A heaviness weighed on the air around them, thick and suffocating. Not even sun or sound could penetrate it.

"Ugh!" Andra cried all of a sudden, startling Kyro and Cypher. "What is this?" She wrinkled her nose as she wiped strange black slime off her shoulder.

Kyro examined it and looked for a source, but saw nothing.

"Did you touch anything recently?" he said.

Andra shivered. "Definitely not. These woods and mountains don't exactly seem friendly. Not like the woods in Drenn."

Homesickness struck Kyro without warning. He missed those woods too. Strange that he could miss both his homes, Romvi and Drenn, at the same time.

"Well, it had to come from something. Keep an eye out," Kyro said.

As they progressed deeper into the mountains, an odd smell clung to the air. Almost like sulfur. The black slime became thicker and more pronounced, coating the trees and branches overhead in dangling gobs until they had to walk stooped to avoid it. Something about the slime and the smell was vaguely familiar to Kyro, but he couldn't recall why. A chilling sense of dread settled deeper into his bones with every step. Andra plodded on without complaint, but one look at her face betrayed the fact that her fears were the same as Kyro's.

They may not be as alone out here as they'd thought.

By midday they were forced to stop and eat a hurried lunch of rolls and cheese. They held their noses the entire time. Cypher ate a few biscuits.

They'd only been sitting for a short while on an old fallen tree trunk—which they had to clear of slime first—when a slight rustling disturbed the air above them. Cypher growled. Andra and Kyro choked down the remains of their food and shoved the rest into their packs.

If something was up there in the trees, they didn't want to meet it. Or to become *its* lunch instead.

As the afternoon marched on, so did they. Their pace began to flag as the daylight faded, darkening the half-light into deeper shades of gray. The shadows of the foreign trees twisted around them, looming larger than before.

"Should we make camp soon?" Andra asked.

Kyro hadn't really considered that. He'd hoped they'd reach the top and his father before evening. It was only late afternoon now, but the darkness was deeper and more tangible here than he'd expected.

"Not yet. But let's keep an eye out for a clearing or somewhere that's a little less…"

"Creepy?" she said.

"Exactly."

A few minutes later, Andra stopped. "Did you hear that?" she asked, frowning.

Kyro began to shake his head, but then he heard it too. That rustling again.

"I hear it now."

"What do you think it is?" she asked.

"I don't want to find out."

Despite the exhaustion seeping into their legs, they picked up the pace. But soon the rustling grew louder, seeming to come from all over the canopy.

"Didn't you say something about the villagers believing demons lived in these mountains?" Andra whispered.

Kyro swallowed hard. "It's just a myth."

Andra gave him a sharp look. "Like the vissla?"

Kyro's face turned a shade of green. "Maybe we should run?"

He didn't need to ask twice. The pair ran headlong up the path, though its narrow width and winding nature slowed their progress. Cypher ran ahead, as usual, and Kyro was surprised to find him just around the next bend, halted in the middle of the path.

"Cypher, what—" Kyro's mouth dropped open.

His dog had stopped because the path was blocked—by a thick web of black slime.

A web...a web... Why was that so familiar to Kyro? What legends had he heard about the Radamaks, aside from them being forbidden?

Before he could puzzle it out, Cypher wheeled around and Andra screamed.

"Above us!"

Kyro's head shot up. Descending on the strands of black

slime was a horde of spiderlike monsters. The smell of sulfur intensified.

Kyro suddenly understood what they were. Vritrax. They were supposed to be extinct, held at bay by the starlight net, just like the vissla. That's why the slime was familiar—his mother had told him tales about these monsters. He shuddered, hypnotized by the closest one and its bottomless iridescent black eyes, getting closer, and closer…

"Snap out of it, Starboy!" Andra grabbed him by the shoulder and pushed him down the path. There was a great rip in the black web. Andra must have done it while Kyro had been caught in the lure of the vritrax.

An awful clicking rose to a fever pitch, punctuated by a blast of heat and horrid stench. Kyro risked a glance behind and was reminded of a detail he'd forgotten—the vritrax breathed fire. The webbing that had stymied them momentarily was now aflame, which explained the occasional scorch marks they'd seen on trees on the trek up.

"I wish your father had mentioned *that* in his notes," Andra said.

When a blast of heat engulfed the tree next to Kyro, he stumbled to his knees. Before he knew what had happened, he was covered in black slime webbing that was choking his breath and lifting him off his feet.

"No!"

He heard Andra cry, but she sounded so far away. He struggled, but the web only got tighter and it was too slippery to gain purchase. But he did his best to thrash and flail and hope.

Suddenly, he heard a rip. Then he was falling. Andra helped him to his feet and dragged him along.

"Hurry, maybe we can lose them in the rocks up ahead," she said.

Once they reached the rocks, the trees thinned and the vritrax slowed. Perhaps they were not as fast on the ground as they were in the air. Whatever the reason, Kyro was grateful for it.

"Is that a tunnel?" Kyro said.

Andra's eyes brightened. "Come on."

They lurched into the tunnel, flattened themselves against the wall, and paused to catch their breath. Cypher huddled against Kyro's legs. The smell of the vritrax was fading, as were its clicking noises, and there were no slime webs here among the rocks. Together, they breathed a sigh of relief and headed deeper into the tunnel.

"What were they?" Andra asked.

"Vritrax. They're supposed to be extinct. But it seems the vissla aren't the only dark things returning now."

"Let's hope your father's well on his way to stopping whoever's stealing those stars then."

Kyro nodded. "If the vritrax are congregating here, maybe whoever's stealing the stars is too."

Andra shivered, and Kyro could see her breath freezing in the air in the dim light. "Why is it so cold in here?" she asked.

Dread froze Kyro's lungs. Frost crept across the tunnel floor toward them, crackling as it advanced.

A vissla was in these tunnels with them.

CHAPTER TWENTY-THREE

DARKNESS SETTLED AROUND THEM LIKE A SUFFOCATING cloak. Kyro's mind raced.

"We have to hurry," Andra whispered, and Cypher whined his agreement.

"Hold on." Kyro searched through his father's rucksack in the faint light until he found what he was looking for. He held up the vial of stardust. "This might help keep the vissla at bay."

Andra's smile glowed. "Good thinking, Starboy."

Without a moment to lose, they ran headlong down the tunnel. A light glimmered far away at the end like a lone star in the night sky, inspiring them to run faster. Kyro gripped the vial of stardust tightly, hoping he wouldn't need to use it. All around the air grew colder, and ice made the path beneath their feet more treacherous, frosting the walls beside them. As they neared the light, Cypher lost his footing completely and sailed toward the exit, yapping in objection.

But as a dark shadow blocked out the light, the dog's yap turned to a whine. Kyro and Andra stopped short, almost slipping too. Only a few feet separated them from fresh air, but now a vissla loomed over them, blocking their path. No wonder the vritrax hadn't chased them into the tunnels—this was the vissla's domain.

Kyro held up the vial of stardust. It had worked when he needed to keep the vissla out, but he wasn't sure he could fight with it. Next to him, Andra's face was determined, despite being etched with fear.

The shadow moved, and ice crackled around it, coating the walls and floor in a thick blanket. Kyro's heart lurched into his throat as Cypher leapt up from where he had been cowering and sank his teeth into the vissla's ragged, black form.

"No!" Kyro cried, but it was too late. The vissla screamed, its arm expanding from the darkness, turning into an icy blade. It tossed Cypher back to the floor and stabbed at him. Cypher twisted away at the last second, but the blade pierced his leg. He let out a yelp of pain and fear.

Kyro hurtled himself forward as Cypher limped toward

his master. He picked the dog up and cradled him in his arms, tears streaming down his cheeks. He couldn't lose him. A haze of grief and fury brewed inside him, and he almost didn't notice when Andra placed herself between him and the vissla.

The evil creature let out a bloodcurdling shriek and brandished its ice blade in the air. A sudden calm fell over Kyro. He gently rested Cypher on the ground, giving him a quick scratch behind the ears. Then Kyro stood beside Andra to face the vissla.

"You should run. It'll attack any second. You need to get to safety."

Andra scoffed. "Run? Are you joking? I'm not going anywhere. Besides, all that's behind us are the vritrax, and I don't want to go through them again either." She shook her head. "No, we're in this together."

Kyro realized her cheeks were also streaked with tears. She always put on a brave face, but Cypher's injury had affected her too.

The vissla shrieked again. Kyro opened the vial of stardust, ready to throw it on the vissla just to see what might happen.

But before the dark creature could attack, a blazing beam of blue light filled the tunnel and swallowed the vissla where it stood.

It screamed with pain, the ice around it melting. As it was

beaten back from the tunnel entrance, Kyro and Andra flattened themselves against the wall. It flew past them in a blast of cold, retreating into the darkest corners of the tunnel.

Kyro and Andra stood in shocked silence. Something had saved them, had banished the vissla, but they had no idea who or what. For a moment, the faint hope that it might be his father returning from the mountains filled Kyro, but it was swiftly replaced by confusion and astonishment.

The sound of metal gears churning rang through the tunnel, sparking their curiosity. Kyro gently picked up Cypher, who whined and nipped at his sleeve, then he and Andra stepped into the light together. It took them a moment to realize what was making the strange noise. The first thing they saw were rusted metal tree trunks, but they soon understood that they were not trees at all: they were legs. Above them was a dented metal torso enclosing a blue orb of light that hummed and spun, likely the source of the light that defeated the vissla. From the shoulders sprouted arms similar to the one they'd found in the desert. And at the very top was a face comprised of metal and gears, and around its neck hung a threadbare red scarf. The giant regarded them with glowing blue eyes and what Kyro hoped was curiosity.

The pair staggered backward as the mechanical giant knelt in front of them, its enormous face coming down to eye level.

"Greetings, friends. The vissla will not trouble you anymore

today." Its voice was like metal scraping stone, but the words were spoken clearly.

Kyro managed to stammer, "Thank you."

Andra's eyes bulged from her head as she stared at the giant. "You're... You're a giant!"

"Of course, I am," the mechanical creature said. "What else would I be?" He made a strange sound that startled them. But it was only the giant's way of laughing. "My name is Jector."

Jector held out his hand, and Kyro and Andra each cautiously took a finger to shake. Several of them were tipped with needles the length of Kyro's forearm.

"I'm Kyro, and I'm looking for my father."

"And I'm Andra. It's very nice to meet you."

"Likewise," said Jector. He gave Kyro a long look, then noticed the injured dog in the boy's arms. "Come with me. I believe I can offer you help with your animal and perhaps your mission as well." Jector held out the palm of his hand, and Kyro gingerly set Cypher in it.

For a brief second, he had the fleeting concern that perhaps the giant might not be as trustworthy as he seemed. He was a stranger, after all. But he had just saved them from the vissla, and the giants had placed the stars in the sky. If there was anyone who should be on their side, it was them.

Trusting Jector seemed like their best option, especially if he could help Cypher. The dog was growing more and more listless. A knot tightened in Kyro's chest, and his heart thumped against it like a drum. He had no idea how else to make his best friend better.

Andra placed a hand on Kyro's shoulder and squeezed as they followed Jector. At first, the giant's huge steps took him too far too fast as he deftly maneuvered through the trees, and they had to run to keep up. But once Jector realized this, he slowed down so they could walk at a normal pace.

"I can't believe we found a real, live giant!" Andra whispered.

Kyro shook his head. "I know. I can't either. Though I'm even more surprised to find one in the Radamak Mountains. All the stories my mother told me were very clear that nothing good lived here."

"Well, the stories can't get everything right, now can they?" She smiled, and Kyro's worries began to melt away. She was right. The mechanical giant was kind and wanted to help. It was best not to question a blessing.

CHAPTER TWENTY-FOUR

KYRO AND ANDRA HAD GROWN TIRED AND HUNGRY, SO when Jector finally stopped, they were relieved. Then they realized where they were.

They had not stumbled upon one lone giant of old; they'd found an entire village of them. An area on the side of the Radamak Mountains had been cleared of trees, and tall houses dotted the landscape in a haphazard fashion. Jector led them straight to the center of the little village where there were several more giants sitting around a firepit.

"There are more of them," Andra murmured quietly in Kyro's ear.

It was almost impossible to imagine that any giants had survived for a thousand years, let alone at least a dozen.

The way Kyro had always imagined them had been far too simplistic. These were not just mindless machines. They moved and spoke among themselves almost like humans. They were living beings, just as much as Kyro and Andra were.

Jector carried Cypher over to another mechanical giant, one that was made of a bright red-tinted metal, striking next to Jector's gray and blue tones. Jector said something to the other giant that Kyro could not make out, but it caused the other giant to take Cypher and carry him into a nearby hut. Kyro's heart stuck in his throat and he moved to follow them, when something else stopped him.

Andra tugged on his arm, her face pale and drawn. Kyro's eyes followed in the direction she was pointing, and his breath halted in his lungs, as if someone had just punched him in the stomach.

There was his father, sitting with the mechanical giants and staring into the blazing firepit. His hair was bedraggled as though he hadn't brushed it in weeks, and his eyes held a terrible vacant look that Kyro didn't like at all. His father absentmindedly fiddled with a gear that was large enough to belong to one of the giants.

"Father," he said, still too far away for Tirin to hear him. Suddenly, all the anger he'd been holding back these last few days rushed into his gut, boiling over. His father hadn't been on some grand mission; he'd been wandering aimlessly and had probably stumbled upon the giants in much the same way they had.

His father had no more of a clue how to save the stars than they did. Yet he'd stayed away from his son and his home. He'd been gone for days. He could have come back and told Kyro about the wondrous giants.

But instead he chose to remain among them.

Kyro's hands balled into fists at his sides. His father really had abandoned him. And all for nothing.

"Don't you want to talk to him?" Andra asked, her brow furrowed.

"Yes...and no. Look at him. He's a mess." Kyro let out an exasperated sigh and did his best to swallow his disappointment and anger.

"He's still your father."

Kyro feared it was in name only now. But Andra was right. He'd found his father; he had to talk to him and convince him to come home and fix things with the Star Shepherd Council. Otherwise, they'd lose everything.

Kyro took a deep breath and headed toward the firepit where his father sat. Out of the corner of his eye, he saw Jector and Andra a little way behind, but he ignored them. He might lose his resolve if anything interrupted him now.

He marched up to his father, blocking his view of the firepit. Tirin didn't even seem to notice; he simply continued his staring and tinkering with the gear in his hands.

"Father?" Kyro said, almost frightened now. What had happened to his father to make him this way? This was a far worse state than Kyro had ever imagined he would find him in.

"Father? It's your son. I've come to bring you home." Still, Tirin made no response. "You have to come home."

Desperation had begun to seep into Kyro's bones when Jector tapped him on the shoulder with one huge pointer finger.

"He will not answer you," Jector said.

All the giants, including Jector, gave Kyro pitying looks. Andra came up beside him and squeezed his hand.

"Well, why not? What's wrong with him? He's my father, but he doesn't even recognize me."

"Then I am very sorry indeed. He is a broken man. We found him not long ago, starving and half-frozen after an encounter with a vissla."

One of the others spoke up too. "We nursed him back to health as best we could, but something happened to him out there in the mountains that shut him off. All he seems to want to do is work on clockwork, which has been a very lucky thing for us." The giant pointed to his metal torso. "That's what we're made of inside, and we are not so easy to fix. But this one, he is very good."

"Yes," Jector nodded. "He has been a great help to us. He understands how we work better than we do."

Kyro suddenly grew light-headed as his stomach turned. "So he's been *here* this whole time, repairing you all?"

The giants nodded, exchanging looks that revealed they didn't quite grasp why Kyro was so upset.

Jector leaned down and asked, "Could you tell us, what is his name? We have taken to calling him the Human, but he does not respond to that."

Ice began to form in Kyro's gut, even worse than the chill of a vissla.

"His name's Tirin," he said. "He was supposed to be out here on an important mission. One he left me behind, alone, to complete." His face had turned as red as frostbite. "It was all for nothing."

Kyro could take no more of the giants' surprised, sad looks. He stormed to the edge of the village, Andra at his heels.

"Kyro!" Andra called, but he kept going. He was ready to leave this mountain, the stars, and even his own father behind. What good had any of it done him? All it had brought was misery.

He didn't have to take it anymore.

Andra grabbed him by the elbow, and he spun around. "Where are you going?" she asked.

"Home." Kyro turned to go back toward the cave, but she blocked his way.

"Are you joking, Starboy?"

"Don't call me that. I hate the stars." Kyro said, though he immediately regretted it. He actually rather liked the nickname Andra had given him. It had made him feel special, as if he had an important job. But now that job had become a burden he couldn't bear. Not alone.

"No, you don't. You're upset because your own father doesn't recognize you. Anyone would be."

"No, I really do hate the stars. I used to think Star Shepherding was a wondrous thing. But the stars made the villagers hate me, and they took my father away from me. They've brought me all the way into the mountains on a fool's errand. I want nothing to do with them ever again." Kyro tried to move past Andra, but she grabbed his arm.

"We came out here not just to find your father, but to do something about the stars. Someone's cutting them down. We need to find out who and stop them." She glanced over her shoulder at Tirin and frowned. "And now that your father's out of commission, that duty falls to us."

Her words softened the edge of Kyro's anger. "What if I don't want that duty anymore?"

"If we don't do something, who will? You told me yourself— most people think the stories about the stars and the vissla are just legends. But we've seen them, we know better. We have to do something."

Kyro closed his eyes, wanting nothing more than to magically be home, safe in the watchtower with everything back to normal. "I don't know if I can do it, Andra. I'm sorry. Everything I've tried so far has been a failure."

"Fine." Now Andra's voice was tinged with irritation. "If you won't save the stars, then I will." She stepped out of Kyro's way and headed back toward the firepit.

Kyro stared, mouth agape, as an awful realization dawned on him at last: nothing would ever go back to normal again. Maybe there'd be a new normal at some point in the future, but the one he'd known was gone. First in Romvi, now in Drenn. He could run away, or he could stand up—with Andra—and be brave.

It was an easier choice than he'd expected.

CHAPTER TWENTY-FIVE

"WAIT!" KYRO RAN AFTER ANDRA, AND SHE TURNED TO him with a knowing smile and a raised eyebrow. "I'm sorry. You're right. Let's talk to Jector. Maybe he knows something."

She grinned wider. "I was just thinking the same thing." She slid her hand into Kyro's, and the warmth of her grip fueled his resolve to save the stars in spite of his father.

"Is it still okay if I call you Starboy?"

Kyro had to smile. What would he have done without her?

"Of course."

Jector ducked into the same house his fellow giant had disappeared into with Cypher, and they followed him, determined to learn what they could from their new friends. But when they stepped inside, they were startled into awed silence.

The interior walls of the house were covered in intricate carvings of stars and constellations and thin lines connecting them in a netlike formation. They were hauntingly lovely and unlike anything Kyro had seen before.

Jector and the other giant were bent over Kyro's dog, who was laid out on a small table. The second giant was smaller than Jector and the needles at the ends of its fingertips were hooked. The giants were working together to patch up Cypher and bind his wounds. The needle tips on their huge hands were somehow able to do this delicate work.

All Kyro's anxiety about Cypher rushed back, making him dizzy. "Will he be all right?"

Jector glanced up from Cypher's still body. "He should be good as new very soon. We're almost done."

"Thank you," Kyro managed to say, warm relief washing over him. If the vissla had succeeded...

Kyro shuddered and banished the thought.

The smaller giant nodded. "We are quite good at fixing flesh creatures, just like we are at making burlap cases. But our own clockwork insides have so often mystified us. Needles are useless for it."

A wayward laugh bubbled up in Kyro's throat, but he swallowed it back. He'd save his laughter for when the stars were all back in the sky and the vissla were once again banished.

"You made the original cases for the stars?" Andra asked.

Jector nodded. "Indeed we did. That is why we were created."

She frowned. "But what have you been doing out here since?"

Jector and the other giant exchanged a glance and shrugged their huge metal shoulders, the resulting creak reverberating through Kyro's teeth.

"Waiting," Jector said.

"Did you make these carvings?" Kyro asked, eyeing the walls of the house.

Jector's clockwork eyebrows lifted. "Why, yes. It helps to pass the time. It is the layout of the stars in the sky and how together they form the starlight net."

"It's a map. How wonderful," Andra said, gazing at the walls with newfound respect.

They finished with Cypher, and to Kyro's immense relief, his dog's chest rose and fell in peaceful sleep. Kyro fished in his pocket for a biscuit and left it near Cypher's nose so he'd find it when he woke up.

"Let me introduce you to the others," Jector said. "First, this is Rumy. She is a Weaver." He gestured to the giant who had helped him patch up Cypher.

"Pleased to meet you," Kyro said. "Thank you for helping my dog."

Andra wrinkled her nose. "What's a Weaver?"

"Most of us here are Stitchers, like me," Jector said, "but others like Rumy are Weavers, and we have a few Framers too."

Rumy said. "We wove the star casings, Stitchers sewed the pieces together, and Framers crafted the hooks to hang them in the night sky. Put a Stitcher and Weaver together, and we can sew up a torn metal body, or a fleshy one. With the help of a Framer, we can make houses, tents, most things we need."

"But you have a hard time with clockwork?" Kyro asked, surprised.

"We do. The gears work together too precisely, and there are too many of them." Rumy held up her hands. While nimble compared to Jector's, they were still quite large. "We cannot get a grip on them, and our needles cannot sew gears back together."

"That is why your father appearing in these mountains has been such a gift. Some of us have been lumbering around broken for decades or longer," Jector said. "We can patch ourselves up fine, but stars help you if you have a broken gear in your knee."

Kyro digested this as Jector led them from the house and introduced them to each of the other giants sitting near the firepit with Tirin. It was difficult not to look at his father and hope that his condition would suddenly change. Every time his father moved, Kyro would glance over, hope rising in his heart, only to have it dashed just as quickly. He tried to focus on the introductions instead, but that was easier said than done and they went by in a blur.

Jector indicated they should sit around the firepit. It was a strange sight—two children and a grown man, surrounded by kneeling mechanical giants chatting like old friends.

Andra made small talk with the giants while Kyro turned to his father. He had to find a way to get through to him somehow.

"Father," he said, this time placing a hand on his shoulder. "Please look at me." But Tirin just continued spinning the gear in his hands. Tears welled up in Kyro's eyes. "Father, the Council has forbidden us from touching the stars. But the stars are in danger. Someone is stealing them. That's why you left me. I don't know what happened to you, but the stars need you. I need you. We're going to lose everything if you don't snap out of this. Please." Kyro's voice cracked on the last word, and he stopped and stared at his father for a few more moments. No reaction. He may as well not even be sitting next to him. He may as well not even exist.

Heaviness fell over him as he turned away from his father. How many times could he get his hopes up before they were crushed beyond repair?

A tap on his knee startled him. His father was facing him, holding out the gear he'd been spinning in his hands. He didn't say a word and his eyes were still lost, but it was something. Kyro took the gear tentatively.

"Father?" he whispered. Tirin grunted and picked up another gear. Kyro sighed and put the gear his father had handed him in his rucksack. It wasn't much, but an acknowledgment of his existence was something at least. He would take what little crumbs he could get.

Jector's voice interrupted Kyro's thoughts. "We are glad the two of you are in better shape than your father. We know that vissla was troubling you, but did you encounter anything else? We were hoping for a clue as to what made Tirin the way he is now." Jector's face, despite being made from metal, managed to look genuinely curious and concerned.

"Oh, we definitely encountered something else." Andra said wryly.

"A horde of vritrax. Fire-breathing spiderlike creatures, with slimy black webbing." Kyro shuddered. "We were fleeing them when we entered the vissla's cave."

"Vritrax?" Jector gasped. The others murmured. "But that is impossible. No one has seen their kind for hundreds of years."

Kyro shrugged. "That's what everyone said about the vissla too."

Rumy leaned forward. "There was an entire horde?"

"Oh yes," Andra said. "They wanted to have us for dinner."

Rumy shook her head gravely. "That does not bode well. For them to be here and so bold is very bad news indeed."

"Have you seen anything strange?" Andra asked.

"Only the vissla and your father. We have heard strange howls and rustlings in these woods, but we mostly keep to ourselves," Jector said.

"Perhaps that was a mistake," Rumy wondered aloud.

"We've seen many strange things," Kyro said. "My father and I are Star Shepherds. It is our sworn duty to protect the stars in the sky and send them back where they belong anytime they fall." He gazed at his hands twisting in his lap. "But something has gone wrong. Someone is stealing the stars. They're being cut down. Whole constellations at once." He rummaged in his bag and held up one of the severed star hooks for all to see. "See? They're not rusted or worn out; they've been sliced. I don't understand who's responsible—or how they've managed it—but it must be the reason creatures like the vritrax and the vissla have been reappearing. There's a hole in the starlight net."

Kyro's throat choked up. The giants had gone silent and exchanged worried looks. Andra put a hand on his arm and picked up the thread of conversation.

"It's why we're here. Kyro's father left home to stop whoever has been stealing the stars. We followed him this far, hoping to help. We have to fix this."

Jector finally spoke. "That is quite a strange tale, though I cannot deny the vissla and the vritrax give it the look of truth. Stolen stars would explain their reappearance." He scratched his metal chin, and it made an odd tinny sound that tickled Kyro's eardrums. "Our little camp is not the only one. We are part of vast army of metal giants. There are the Orers who mined the ore, the Crafters who made the hearts of stars, and the Flyers who hung the stars in the sky. I do not know who else would be able to reach the stars, but I cannot imagine any of them would be to blame."

Several of the others scoffed and snorted metallically. Jector frowned at them, but Rumy spoke anyway.

"Our job as Stitchers was vitally important, but some of the others have grown too big for their metal britches, if you ask me. The Flyers deemed themselves more important, and we were ostracized from our brothers and sisters. That was when we came here so we could go about our business as we see fit."

"Wait, the ones who actually hung the stars in the sky are still around?" Andra said in disbelief.

"Of course. We all are."

"But we thought you died out. Everyone did," Kyro said. "When we found you, we assumed you were all that was left."

"And we thought you all could fly," Andra added.

Rumy and several others laughed, sending a ringing rhythm toward the stars. "Lucky for us, we do not die that easily. And we are happy enough on the ground."

Kyro glanced at Andra and knew without question that she was thinking the very same thing he was.

"We need you to take us to see them. We have to talk to the flying giants."

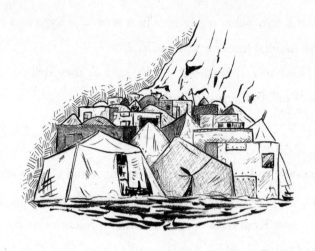

CHAPTER TWENTY-SIX

IT TOOK SOME CONVINCING, BUT KYRO AND ANDRA finally persuaded Jector and Rumy to bring them to where the rest of their army was encamped in the mountains the next morning. But before they settled in for the night in the Stitchers' camp, Kyro checked on Cypher, only to have his dog bound out of the house yapping and pawing at his master's knees in greeting. Kyro threw his arms around Cypher's neck.

"Good boy," he whispered. "I'm so glad you're all better."

When Kyro curled up to sleep on the floor of Jector's house, Cypher snuggled up beside him. His father snored nearby, but so far the only acknowledgment he'd shown of Kyro was when he had handed him the gear earlier.

"Don't worry, Starboy," Andra said as they drifted off to sleep. "We'll find answers in the morning."

>~◎ ⊙~<

When they woke the next day, Jector suggested Cypher remain at the camp to continue recuperating, but he refused to leave Kyro's side. Kyro didn't mind; Cypher's presence was comforting and helped hold back the unsettling reminder of his father's continued absence, now only in spirit though not in body.

Jector and Rumy led them onto the path between the trees and lumbered ahead, occasionally talking down toward them.

"Be warned, not all giants are fond of humans. I have always liked them, but it took Tirin's arrival to convince the rest of our little group that humans are fine creatures." Jector cleared his throat, and it sounded like rocks clanging. "You may not be welcomed there."

"Indeed," Rumy said. "We might not be either."

"It's all right," Kyro said. "It's our only lead, so it's worth the risk."

"Do they really dislike you that much?" Andra asked.

The mechanical giants exchanged a look. "I am afraid they do. Their general, Sear, has long held a grudge against us. He believes our work to be of little importance," Jector said.

"And he did not appreciate the fact the Seven Elders did not see things the same way," Rumy said. "Once long ago, they put Jector in charge. But everything changed after their sacrifice."

Jector fiddled with his red scarf. "Yes, one of the Elders gave me this scarf. I have not taken it off since. Once it marked me as the leader, though now it means little to anyone except me."

"With the Elders gone, Sear and his captains threw out all the Stitchers and Weavers and Framers and anyone else who sided with Jector openly," Rumy said.

Andra patted the back of Jector's metal leg. "I'm sorry. That's terrible. But they'll have to listen to us. They can't ignore something that involves the stars, I'm sure."

Jector and Rumy didn't look quite as certain as Andra sounded, but they said nothing to contradict her. The forest around them grew darker as the day waned, the ancient tall trees of the Radamaks looming above them like monsters waiting to pounce. But with two giants on their side, Kyro felt braver than he had before, and he could tell Andra did too. With every step they took, his resolve solidified. There was much more to discover about the stars in the mountains. Even if the culprit couldn't be found here, perhaps the solution would. Surely, if the Flyers who originally hung the stars heard about someone stealing them, they could be persuaded to help. Maybe they'd even hang new stars to replace the stolen ones and banish the vissla and vritrax to the prison behind the star-light net for good.

Yes, the answer was hidden in these dark, dangerous hills. He and Andra only had to find it.

They'd hiked for what felt like miles when Jector and Rumy began to mumble over their heads. Kyro couldn't make out what they were saying, but the giants' tone didn't sound happy.

"What's wrong?" Kyro asked. But before they could answer, something huge swooped out of the sky and lifted Jector by his arms, carrying him toward the tops of the trees.

"Stop!" Andra cried, running after their new friend without hesitation, before even Rumy reacted. Kyro had no doubt what the something was—one of the Flyers—though he was startled by its behavior. He and Cypher caught up with Rumy and Andra in a clearing of tall obsidian rocks that jutted up from the ground in sharp points. Jector and the interloper hovered over the center of the clearing.

The Flyer did not seem friendly.

"Put him down!" Andra yelled, folding her arms over her chest, but the Flyer paid her no attention.

Jector's voice floated down to them. "Sear, we mean no trouble, I promise."

The Flyer—Sear—scowled, his glowing yellow eyes flashing through the slits in his metal face.

"You were warned not to return to our camp. We do not

want your kind here. And to bring those filthy humans too! You know the consequences." Sear prepared to release Jector over the pointed rocks, but paused when Rumy yelled up at him.

"These humans need to speak to Pelag. That is all," she said.

"We only need a few minutes of his time, and then we will be on our way, never to bother you again. I swear on the stars," Jector said.

"What business do they have with Pelag?"

Rumy put her metal hands on her hip joints. "They are Star Shepherds. They wish to discuss a matter concerning the stars with him."

A strange new light gleamed in Sear's eyes. "The stars? That ought to be interesting." He flew down and alighted on the ground, dropping Jector unceremoniously but safely between the trees at the edge of the clearing. "I'll bring you to Pelag. You will have only a few minutes of his time, and then you must go on your way, never to return. If I see any of you"—he glowered at Kyro and Andra too—"here again, I will not be so generous. Come along. Quickly."

They hurriedly agreed. Sear stood a good two feet taller than Jector and with broader shoulders. Hulking arms hung down, almost vibrating with hidden strength. His face was a blank sheet of dark metal, except for the glowing yellow slits that served as eyes. Everything about him suggested power, speed, and impatience.

Airborne, Sear was far faster than Andra and Kyro could ever hope to be. Jector and Rumy scooped each of them up so the giants could walk with longer strides to keep pace. Kyro clung to Cypher in his arms. In mere minutes, they reached a plateau not far from the peak of the mountain and the rest of the camp.

Kyro and Andra gaped. The main camp dwarfed Jector's camp in size. Everywhere they looked, there were tall houses and tents and mechanical giants flying to and fro through the air. It was a bustling city in comparison to Jector's small encampment.

Jector sighed. "I do not miss this place. The peace and quiet of our camp is vastly preferable." Rumy nodded her agreement.

The giants did not seem to have missed Jector or Rumy either. Skeptical looks and wary glances followed them. But Sear must have been important; no one troubled them.

Kyro shivered. If Sear disliked humans so much, what would the leader think of them? Kyro had been hopeful this Pelag would help, but their greeting by the Flyers didn't inspire confidence. Jector had warned them the Flyers wouldn't be friendly, but Sear's reaction to Jector seemed extreme, to say the least.

Sear led them to the center of the camp and a house that was shorter than the others around it, but much wider as though to make up for it. Sear landed and knocked on the roof at the same time Jector and Rumy reached the house. They set Kyro and Andra on the ground, then Jector shifted from foot to foot nervously. His behavior had grown stranger the closer they'd gotten to the center of the camp, and Kyro couldn't help but wonder why. Rumy seemed more suspicious of the others than anything else.

The door opened, and out stepped the very last thing Kyro had expected to see in the Flyer camp.

An ancient man, stooped over a cane, with long hair that was a shocking white and a beard down to his knees.

"Yes, Sear, what is—" He stopped midsentence when he saw Kyro and Andra. "Who are you? Why did you bring them here, Sear?"

The light flickered in Sear's eyes. "They are Star Shepherds, Pelag, and they wish to talk to you about the stars."

The man grew still, regarding them for a moment with suspicion. "Well, all right. Since you came all this way. Come in."

There was no room for the mechanical giants in this house, but Jector gave Kyro and Andra a nudge to follow the man inside. Kyro didn't feel right leaving him and Rumy behind when the Flyers clearly didn't like them, but his curiosity was far too great.

The inside of the house was an extraordinary assortment of machinery, some of it clockwork, some of it not. Along the far side, a bed suspended by metal poles began to wind back

into the wall to give them more room. There was a kitchen area, with some strange machines whose function Kyro couldn't hazard to guess, except the cold box that clicked and clanked. The center of the room had a couple chairs and a couch, circling another odd machine. It whirred and puffed warm steam into the air. Kyro had never seen anything like it. A pang struck him. His father would have loved this.

"Where did you get all this?" Kyro asked. "Are you a clockmaker?"

Pelag snorted and took a seat on a chair. It had gears that turned at the touch of a button to lift his legs off the floor on an extra section of cushion. Kyro sat across from him on the couch, and Andra eyed it warily before joining him.

"Well, what is it you want?" Pelag huffed.

"We've come into the Radamak Mountains in search of help. My father and I are Star Shepherds, and a few weeks ago we discovered that someone is cutting down the stars. They're being stolen, though we do not know why."

Pelag shrugged. "So? What does it matter if the stars fall? Isn't it your job to put them back?"

Kyro and Andra exchanged a surprised look. Of all people, they had thought a man who lived with giants would understand the ramifications.

"Yes, and we do—when we can find them. But someone else is taking the stars after they fall before we can get to them. The stars hold back dark, terrible creatures. They're returning now that there are holes in the starlight net."

Pelag laughed, then coughed. "Sounds like another Shepherd is encroaching on your territory. You just need to be faster. That is all."

"That isn't it. I've seen the vissla myself," Kyro objected.

"Stars are dying. Shouldn't this worry you?" Andra asked, exasperated at Pelag's lack of reaction. "You're the leader of the giants, and they're the ones who hung the stars in the first place!"

Pelag examined the knob of his cane, then sighed. "That was a very, very long time ago. For all we know, the dark creatures have all died out by now. And what proof have you that stars are dying? Why should I believe the word of children when I have been alive for so long and seen so much more than you?"

Cold trickled over Kyro's spine. "But we're telling the truth."

Pelag glared. "Why should I believe that? I bear no love for Star Shepherds, boy. You served a purpose once, but that need has long since faded away."

Andra shot to her feet. "What are you saying?"

Pelag smiled and held out his hands. "You said you seek the one cutting down the stars? Well, you have found him."

Kyro's throat constricted, and Cypher growled at his feet. "But that doesn't make any sense. Why would you want to do that? How?"

Pelag sat up in his chair, lowering his feet back to the floor with a grinding of gears.

"Many centuries ago, the secrets of the Elders lived only with a small group of us. People had stopped believing the stars kept evil away. There was no one left to pass our knowledge on to, so we attached a portion of our hearts to those within the stars." He pulled aside his robe to show Kyro a jagged scar on his chest. "We were trying to prolong our lives, and it worked. The power of the stars allowed us to live indefinitely. But after many years the burden became too much to bear. As our loved ones passed on, we remained. Slowly growing older and frailer, but still here. Still attached to this life because of the stars."

Kyro sucked his breath in sharply at the same time Andra's jaw dropped. His head spun. A descendant of the Elders, alive and living in the Radamak Mountains? No wonder Pelag was the leader. Had his father stumbled upon this information as well? Could that have been the final bread crumb that convinced him to brave the forbidden mountains?

If Pelag noticed their reaction, he gave no sign of it as he continued with his tale. "Then, one of our group's stars fell, and as it perished, so did he. We were finally content in the knowledge that our time would expire with that of the stars we were attached to. Though we had none to pass our knowledge to, we believed the ancient evils to be extinct. That was the purpose of the starlight net—to banish them so deep into the darkest corners that they couldn't survive. Centuries had passed. There was no longer anything left to fear, and I looked forward to finally being released from this world.

"But this was around the time the first Star Shepherds emerged, and they ruined my hopes for peace." Pelag's hands clenched around his cane like he wanted to strangle it. "My star fell, but it was rescued and shot back into the sky. As the others of my group passed on, I found my way to these mountains, where the giants have kept me company. But I am tired, so tired, and I need to move on from this life. Once, I gave up everything for the stars. Now I will search every star in the sky if I have to in order to find the peace I deserve."

"You can't do that!" Kyro said. "What about the Elder Stars? What about keeping us safe and keeping the darkness out?"

Pelag laughed. "As I said, that time has passed. For all we know, the Elder Stars have fallen as well. And you Star Shepherds return the stars to the sky anyway. What does it matter if we cut some down to find mine?"

"Because they're not going back into the sky! Someone is stealing them."

Pelag shook his head. "Like I said, what proof have you of this? Besides, whatever evil existed then is long gone. It doesn't matter if a few stars go astray. I have waited and watched for centuries to be sure."

"But the evil *isn't* gone!" Kyro argued. "We saw vritrax and a vissla on our way here in these very mountains. The stars that have been destroyed are making them braver."

"Enough! I grow weary of your childish tales. You will not deter me with your lies. The stars are fine. My giants are only looking for the one with my heart. The Shepherds take care of the rest."

Resolve filled Kyro with a swift urgency. "We're telling the truth. Something or someone is taking them before the Shepherds can get to them. We'll shoot your giants out of the sky if we have to," he said. "We won't let you do this."

"I am afraid you have no choice," Pelag said, his eyes boring into Kyro. "If I have to personally lead my army to your doorstep, I will not hesitate to do so."

The old man rose to his feet. "I believe you have what you came for. An answer. And now you have overstayed your welcome." He gestured toward the door.

Andra looked like she had swallowed a hive of bees, but she and Kyro did as they were told. Outside, they found Jector waiting for them. Pelag instructed Sear, "Be sure they leave the camp immediately. And that they do not return." He turned to Kyro and Andra. "I wish I could say it has been a pleasure, but as I mentioned, I bear no fondness for Star Shepherds."

With that, Pelag ducked back into his house, and they were left with a sneering Sear and several more Flyers glaring down at them.

CHAPTER TWENTY-SEVEN

THE FLYERS CORRALLED THE GROUP, MOVING THEM along the edge of the camp and back toward the mountain path. Sear shoved Jector forward. "You heard Pelag. Time to leave. And never come back."

"This isn't right." Andra glared up at Sear as he nudged her along too. "You're helping Pelag, aren't you? You're stealing the stars for him. Why are you destroying them in the process? Why even bother cutting them down when you could just take them?"

Kyro's heart sank. One look at Sear left no doubt she was right. Of course the Flyers were in on it. It explained so much—the speed with which the stars were stolen, the hooks in the desert. But were they all, or just Sear and his captains?

And why *were* they cutting down the stars? It made no sense. If they could reach them, there was no point in slicing the hooks or the burlap. They could have just taken them, and the Star Shepherds would have been none the wiser until it was too late.

Some of the other Flyers frowned, then laughed. "That's ridiculous," one said. "We hung the stars. Why would any of us take them down again?"

"You should not discuss things you know nothing about," Sear hissed. "Or there might be repercussions." His face bent low enough that Kyro and Andra could both feel the cold breath of the mechanical giant blowing over their faces.

Jector stepped between them and the three foremost Flyers. "Now, Sear, Boor, Aranxes, there is no need to threaten these two human children. They only came here to help."

Sear pushed a finger into Jector's chest, the sound ringing in Kyro's ears. The other two Flyers took a step closer. "If I see a need, then there is one. You do not get a say."

Jector's metal hands clenched and unclenched in a clockwork rhythm. "Leave them alone."

"No." Sear shoved Jector into the gathered Flyers behind them, and the giant stumbled backward, only to be propelled forward by the others, who cackled and jeered at him.

"Ha! Poor Jector. No propulsion to keep his balance and stay upright," Boor said. He was as tall and sleek as Sear, but his chest plate was rusted through in some places.

"Fool." Aranxes laughed, and the other Flyers and a few larger, hulking giants Kyro guessed were Orers laughed with him.

Jector launched himself at Sear. Cypher yapped, but none of the giants noticed the dog while Jector and Sear tussling held their attention.

Rumy leaned over and whispered, "What happened in there?"

Kyro balled his hands into fists. "Pelag is searching for his heart. He directed Sear and his captains to take down the stars and search them. But he refused to believe us when we told him the stars were being destroyed in the process. He wouldn't take the word of children over Sear."

Andra crossed her arms over her chest. "We need real proof."

Rumy nodded. "It is very strange that Sear would do that. I always thought he was a dedicated giant, though I never liked him personally. He certainly has changed since I last saw him. Pelag is right—you do need proof. No one will believe you otherwise. This is the perfect distraction. Let's sneak back into the camp. Maybe we can find something more about Pelag's plan and prove to the rest of the camp that Sear is helping him cut down the stars." She eyed Sear nervously. "And maybe even letting them die."

"Let's go." Kyro grabbed Andra's hand, and they ran away from the group, Cypher close behind them.

Rumy seemed to know where she was going, and she was small enough to escape the notice of Sear's army now that they were distracted.

"It has been decades since I have set foot in this camp," she said. "But I know someone who might be able to help. While most of the Crafters, Orers, and Flyers think our type of giant beneath them, Rekton never did. Indeed, he still brings us supplies to patch ourselves up once in a while. He might know what is going on."

Rumy led them through the camp, filled with shacks and tents far taller than the ones in Jector's camp. The settlement spread throughout the entire plateau, and Kyro wondered if perhaps no one had never noticed it before because the tents gave it a pointed appearance from a distance. Rumy brought them to a part of the camp that was near a side of the mountain pockmarked by caves.

"This is where the Orers live," she said. "They tunneled into the mountain to get the ore to craft the star hearts and the metal for the hooks."

No giants hung around outside, much to Kyro's relief. The last thing they needed was to get kicked out of the camp for a second time. Rumy went right up to one shack and knocked. The creature who opened the door was impressive even by giant standards. Rekton was as tall as the Flyers, but had huge, thick arms, with heavy gauntlets at the ends, no doubt the better to tunnel with. Like the others, he too had a glowing blue orb in his torso and his eyes flared with life.

"Rumy?" Rekton said. "What are you doing here? And with humans too? It is not safe."

Rumy glanced behind her. "Can we come in? I would not be here if it was not of great importance."

Rekton frowned, his clockwork eyebrows clicking, but held the door wide. The inside of the shack was sparsely furnished, but one wall held various metal tools on hooks that Kyro could only guess must have aided in their tunneling work. A few chairs and a table sat in the middle of the room, but he and the others were in too much of a hurry to sit down.

"Rekton, this is Kyro and Andra. Kyro is a Star Shepherd. He and his father take care of the stars that fall from the sky and send them back to keep the starlight net intact."

"Yes," Rekton said, "I am aware of the Shepherds."

"But," Rumy continued, "recently someone has been cutting down the stars and stealing them. Kyro and Andra spoke to Pelag, but he didn't believe them. We suspect Sear has something to do with it. He has always been gruff, but he seems to have grown cruel now. We know he's helping Pelag, but we don't know why he'd want to hurt the stars."

Rekton didn't seem as surprised by this as Kyro had

expected. Instead, the great giant sighed. "Something has changed in Sear, it is true. And Pelag. He is obsessed with leaving this world. I fear he might go to great lengths to do so."

"That is exactly what he told us. He admitted to cutting down the stars. But he didn't believe that they were being destroyed," Kyro said.

Rekton stroked his chin, considering. "Sear and his captains have been disappearing a lot at night lately. A few weeks ago, a friend of mine confided in me that he suspected they might be hiding something. He told me he planned to fly after them and find out what they were up to, but since that night, no one has seen or heard from him. They almost certainly had something to do with it."

Kyro's head throbbed, and he exchanged a nervous look with Andra. "We found something on the way here, in the Ergsada Valley. It was the arm of a giant. It looked like it had been torn off. It was surrounded by sliced star hooks. At the time, we assumed it had been there for centuries, but now..."

"Yes," Rekton said, his eyes glowing brighter. "That must be my friend, Arctus."

"We need proof Sear and his captains are stealing the stars," Rumy said. "Can you help us?"

"If you need proof, you're bound to find it in their huts."

"Can you show us where Sear's is?" Rumy asked.

Rekton shrugged. "Why not? They have never liked me

much anyway. And I have been thinking it might be time for me to leave this camp behind. I would not mind taking them down a peg or two first."

After checking that the coast was clear outside his shack, Rekton led them across the camp, this time right to the very heart of the sector where the flying giants lived. The deeper they went, the more nervous Kyro became. If they were caught here, their odds of escape were not good at all. But they needed proof to stop Sear, to convince Pelag and the giants who had not yet gone rogue that this was wrong.

Rekton finally stopped in front of the largest shack Kyro had seen. Of course, it would belong to Sear. It rose in front of them, an odd mess of wood and forged metal with a few gears here and there for good measure.

"Show-off," Rumy murmured under her breath. With her needle-hooked fingers, Rumy made short work of the lock on Sear's door, and they slipped inside. Odds and ends of all kinds filled the space, though Kyro wasn't sure what they were, aside from being made from more gears and wood and rocks.

Rekton shrugged. "The Crafters have not had much else to do but Pelag and Sear's bidding lately. Keeps them busy, I suppose."

"And from noticing what Sear is really up to," Andra added, frowning.

"No doubt," Kyro agreed. "Look at this." In the center of the main room there was a long table overflowing with marked-up star maps. The first few Kyro pored over didn't look familiar, but when he got to the middle of the table, there was one in a place of prominence with a particular sector circled.

Kyro's breath fled his lungs. He recognized a constellation that had been crossed out—it was the very one that had fallen the night he and his father finally realized that the stars were indeed being stolen. They had wondered how the stars could have possibly disappeared so quickly, and here was the definitive answer: the flying giant had cut them down and flown them away, leaving only those stark empty craters in their wake.

"This map," Kyro said. "It's the sky right over my watchtower."

Rumy picked up another map nearby. "It looks like these have been cast aside. Pelag has narrowed down the search for his star to your part of the sky. That's where he'll focus his army next."

Kyro shivered. "This is it. This is proof."

Rekton shook his huge head. "Not enough. It is not unusual for us to have star maps, especially our captain."

Kyro's heart sank as he realized Rekton was right. But Andra grinned and squeezed his hand.

"They took those stars. I'll bet you there's a trace of them here somewhere," she said, glancing around. "Let's keep looking."

"Hurry," Rekton warned. "Sear will notice you have snuck off soon. They will be hunting for you."

They split up, each of them taking one room of the shack

and searching it carefully, leaving no piece of clockwork or odd contraption unturned. Kyro looked through what appeared to be a tool room of some kind, filled with all sorts of strange metallic devices, perhaps once used to help craft or hang the stars. But before he even got halfway through the mess, Andra yelled from the main room.

"Come quick! I've got our proof."

Kyro and the others rushed to see what she had found. Andra held up an empty star casing in each hand—both with an unmistakable slice instead of the usual jagged tear.

"There's a whole bunch more in there too." She led them into the room, revealing the closet she'd found where they had been stashed. It was overflowing with burlap sacks just like the ones Andra held. At the bottom were the black, burnt-out husks of star hearts. Rumy gasped, her metal features creaking into a frown.

Kyro put a hand against the wall to steady himself. It was suddenly a little harder to breathe, as though something tight was constricting around his rib cage. So many dead stars. Pelag and Sear must have been at this for months at least. The starlight net was much more damaged than Kyro had ever imagined.

All these irreplaceable stars. Gone.

"There's something very strange going on with Sear," Andra said.

Kyro managed to find the words to speak. "Agreed. Pelag is

a fool and willfully blind. But Sear... This is just vicious behavior. How could a giant who helped hang the stars do this?"

"It's like he's just grown evil over time," Andra said. Kyro nodded. *Evil* was just the right word for it.

Rekton hung his head. "This is very bad indeed," he said. "Very, very bad."

CHAPTER TWENTY-EIGHT

ARMED WITH THE BURLAP SACKS AND A FEW SHELLS of star hearts, Kyro, Andra, and their new friends hurried back to where they'd left Jector tangling with Sear. He was being held up by Sear's captains, and Sear was shouting at him. A huge crowd of giants of all kinds had gathered around them.

"Where did they go? Is this why you returned to the camp—to ruin everything?"

Jector held his head up defiantly, but a few loose bolts hung off his torso.

Andra's face twisted and she barreled into the clearing,

holding the burlap casings up high. "The only one ruining everything is you, Sear! Let Jector go!"

Sear's eyes flashed. "What is it you think you have there?"

Several of the other Flyers murmured.

"We found these in your home. Look," she said, pointing to the slice in the casings. "These stars didn't fall from normal wear and tear; they were cut down on purpose. And then left to die." In her other hand she held up the fragile black husk of a burnt-out star.

Mechanical gasps rang out, though just as many of the giants didn't seem the least bit surprised. Kyro's pulse throbbed in his throat. His hope that only Sear and his captains were embroiled in Pelag's scheme grew fainter by the second.

Sear shook his head. "You must have planted those. We don't trust the word of humans. You cannot prove a thing."

Rekton and Rumy stepped forward. "It is true," Rekton said in a rumbling growl. "I was there when the human girl found them in your house. I have no reason to lie."

Sear's eyes flashed brighter, and he went deadly still. "You ought to carefully consider your words, Rekton. Else they be your last."

"Did you say the same to Arctus? He caught you stealing the stars, and you destroyed him for it," Rekton said, his gauntlets raised.

"Sear!" cried one of the Flyers. "Is this true? Why would

you harm the stars? That is our primary function—to protect them."

"And what's this about Arctus?" yelled another.

Before Sear could answer, Kyro spoke up. "Pelag. He wants to die. And he's determined to cut down every star until he finds the one bearing his heart so he can be released. Sear has been aiding him."

Sear stalked toward Kyro. "I have had just about enough of you intruders—" But before he could finish, a wall of mechanical giants blocked his path.

"These are grave charges, Sear. We take them seriously," said one.

"Go to his house," Andra said. "You'll find more where these came from."

"Until we determine the truth, you are not going anywhere." The giant turned to the one next to him. "Carus, go to Sear's house to verify or defy these claims."

Carus soared into the air without hesitation, leaving a blast of hot steam in his wake.

"You cannot keep me here," Sear said, shoving his way through the wall and readying his boosters to fly. But before he could take off, several giants grabbed him and held him down. Sear struggled, in the process kicking up the burlap casings Andra had set on the ground. They scattered around the clearing. He also knocked over the bag of dead stars, and a glint caught Kyro's eye. Curiosity insisted he pick it up. He ducked flailing metal arms and legs, but he reached the sack and freed the object—a small metal lantern, glowing with a mysterious light.

Before he could examine it properly, Sear yelled. "Put that down! Thief!"

Startled, Kyro quickly shoved the lantern in his pack. Sear lunged for him, but Kyro dodged. Rekton blocked Sear's path, towering over him.

The hum of a Flyer over their heads made everyone look up. Carus settled down among them with a resigned expression on his face. "The humans tell the truth. Sear has many star casings and dead stars in his possession."

The giants who had been holding Jector suddenly let go, and he ran toward Kyro. Sear attempted to shoot up over Rekton to reach Kyro, but Rekton caught him by the foot and Sear came crashing back down to the ground. The clanging metal sent ripples resonating into Kyro's bones. Sear rose to his feet and dusted himself off, growling.

"You will not hurt the boy. You have done quite enough," Rekton said.

Sear shoved Rekton, but he barely budged. "I will do as I please," Sear said. "And so will the rest of the camp." More giants began to appear, until too soon those who sided with Kyro and Andra were outnumbered.

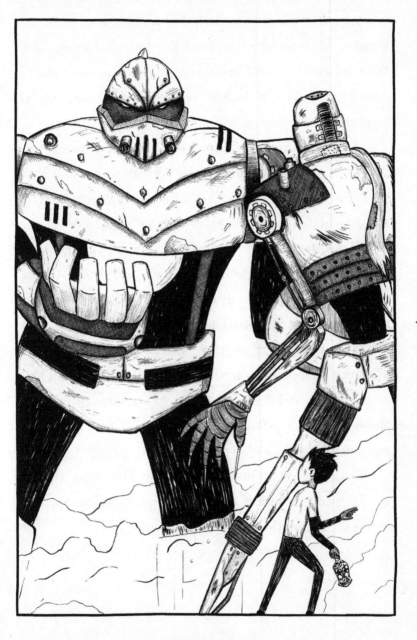

Sear yelled for them to catch the intruders, even while the members of their camp who knew the truth tried to convince them Sear had betrayed their reason for existence. But it was to no avail. Unfriendly metal arms reached for Kyro, until he and Cypher were scooped up by Rekton.

"Your friend is right. There is something very wrong with Sear. He seems to be malfunctioning. We must get you to safety."

Kyro glanced behind to see that Andra had been rescued by a Flyer, and that Rumy and Jector were not far behind.

"If that map we found is any indication, Pelag is going to cut down all the stars near my watchtower in Drenn. We must protect that sector. And to do that, we need to go to Daluth and convince the Star Shepherd Council to help."

"Then we shall get you there with all speed," Rekton said. The great lumbering giant paused to hand off Kyro to a Flyer named Elktor and Andra to Carus. "Take them to the Star Shepherd Council in Daluth. The rest of us will head for Drenn, and you can catch up to us there."

Elktor nodded his head and rumbled. Then, Kyro's stomach dropped into his feet as he and the giant shot into the sky, sailing high above the trees.

CHAPTER TWENTY-NINE

WITH THE HELP OF THEIR NEW FRIENDS, KYRO AND Andra left the Radamak Mountains much faster than the way they had come.

While Jector and his Stitchers headed for Drenn and the watchtower with Tirin, the Flyers who had defected from the main camp carried Kyro and Andra to Daluth and the Star Shepherd Council's watchtower. If they wanted any chance of defeating Pelag and his army, they needed to convince the Council to help and alert the rest of the Star Shepherds.

Thanks to the maps they'd found, they knew exactly where Pelag planned to strike—the sector of the sky over Drenn. Every

Star Shepherd across the lands would need to pledge their aid and their catapults.

Flying was not what Kyro had expected. When he was a little boy, he'd often wondered what it had been like to hang the stars, to fly so high and carry out such an important task. Now he only wondered how some of the giants like Sear had been convinced to abandon that grand mission. Perhaps they were all just malfunctioning as Rekton had suggested. But here he was, clutching Cypher—whose nose was firmly buried in Kyro's chest—and soaring through the air, held fast in the cage of a giant's metal hand. The wind whipped around him, tearing at his hair and jacket. Andra was not far away, and he suspected her thoughts echoed his. A look of elation was clear on her face as she gripped the mechanical fingers holding her safe.

Below them, the Black Sands—so intimidating up close— seemed like nothing more than a smudge on the landscape. Drenn was behind them, and to the west the ocean swirled endlessly to the horizon.

But the best part was above them.

Here, the stars were brighter than ever before, each one sparkling in a unique tone and manner. Kyro was still far enough away that he couldn't see the hooks holding them up, but he could just make out the difference between the older ones with the burlap sacks made by Jector and his kind and the newer casings he and the other Star Shepherds used. Invisible from the ground, but not from this height, thin bands of starlight radiated from star to star, connecting them all. Here and there were patches of hollow darkness where a star had once hung and no longer did.

Something heavy and determined swelled in Kyro's chest.

This was the starlight net. From here, it was easy to see how the vissla and other dark things had been able to escape their dark prisons. The starlight net needed mending, and Kyro had to do it. It was his sworn duty as a Star Shepherd.

He wished the Council leader, Kadmos, could see this. It might very well change his mind.

Then, as the Council's magnificent watchtower came into view, Kyro smiled. He knew just what to do.

>~⊙ ⊙~<

When Elktor, the Flyer who had carried him here, set him down in front of the watchtower door, Kyro nearly laughed. The giant was half as tall as the watchtower itself. If the Council wasn't impressed by him and Carus, the giant carrying Andra, nothing could do it.

"Wait here," Kyro said, and the giants nodded. Andra gazed up in awe at the massive watchtower with its vast number of telescopes dotting the roof.

"Hurry, Kyro," Elktor said. "It has been a long time since I have flown so high. The starlight net is in tatters. We must act now, or it will be too late."

A hard knot formed in Kyro's gut, but he understood. He knocked on the door to the watchtower much more confidently than he had the first time he had come here.

Kyro was just about to knock again when the door opened. "Jakris!" Kyro cried. "I'm so glad to see you."

Jakris frowned in the doorway, glancing from Kyro to Andra and then down at Cypher as the dog wagged his tail and sniffed the man's feet in greeting. "Kyro, you cannot be here. The Council has banned you and your father—"

Jakris's voice choked off as Elktor stepped into view.

"The Council was wrong," Andra said triumphantly.

"And we have the giants to prove it," Kyro said.

Jakris stepped outside, his mouth hanging open. "Impossible," he said breathlessly.

Elktor knelt down and extended a mechanical finger in greeting. "I am Elktor," he said. "The stars have been stolen, and we require the aid of all Star Shepherds immediately."

Jakris put his hand on the extended finger, his own dwarfed by the giant's. He ogled the craftwork of the giant and then peered into his face, fascinated by the glowing blue light behind Elktor's eyes.

"Absolutely extraordinary."

Elktor stood and gestured to the skies behind him.

"Hurry, my brothers and sisters are on their way, ready to be dispatched to Star Shepherds across the world to bring them and their catapults back to Drenn."

Jakris gaped at the metal forms now dotting the sky and growing bigger every few moments. "Wait here. I'll be right back."

He hurried off, leaving them waiting outside to greet the new arrivals.

The others had landed by the time Jakris returned with several members of the Council including Kadmos. Kyro's stomach tightened when he saw the man's scowling face. If anyone would find a reason not to help them, it would be him. Kadmos's robes swept across the doorway as he marched outside.

"What is the meaning of this? Has your father sent you?" He stopped short when he realized they were surrounded by looming mechanical giants. His eyes narrowed. "Is this some sort of trick?"

Jakris sighed behind him, but the other Council members gasped and pushed forward.

"It's no trick, sir," Kyro said. "I went looking for my father, and I found him staying with a group of mechanical giants. They're still alive after all this time. And we all need to work together to save the stars."

Kadmos scoffed. "This again?" He waved a hand and moved to go back inside. "Your father would do anything to regain his status as a Star Shepherd. But all his smoke and mirrors will not change a thing. He abandoned his post and the stars, and the Council's verdict is final." He turned, but had only taken a single step toward the door when Elktor's hand swooped down and pinched the back of his robes, preventing him from going any farther.

"This is not a trick," Elktor rumbled. The other Council members took a large step back, eying the dozen or so giants warily. "We hung the stars, and now some of our brothers have gone astray, convinced by one of the Elders' descendants to cut the stars down. Pelag gave his heart to the stars centuries ago to ensure the knowledge he possessed lived on. But now he is weary of his long life and has become obsessed with finding the star that carries his heart and destroying it so he might leave this life. And he will cut down every star in the sky if he has to in order to achieve his goal."

Andra stepped forward. "You all swore to protect the stars. You didn't believe that anyone could cut them down, but now Kyro has brought you proof. You must protect them."

The Council members murmured, but Kadmos's face had gone pale. "Did you say Pelag?" he whispered.

Elktor nodded, sending a breeze at the group of Star Shepherds.

"He is in our history books, the most ancient of them, along with several others named as the Elders' heirs. It is written that he and the other heirs pledged their lives to ensure the knowledge that was eventually given to the Star Shepherds survived. Indeed, Pelag was one of the very ones who helped us found the Council and suggested the building of our towers and catapults." Kadmos's hands shook. "No one but a Star Shepherd with access to our histories should know about him."

"Or a giant," Kyro said.

Kadmos gazed at him with new eyes, then at his fellow Council members. "We will help you."

CHAPTER THIRTY

KADMOS WAS TRUE TO HIS WORD. HE AND THE OTHER Council members quickly supplied the mechanical giants with directions to the rest of the Star Shepherds.

Kyro and Andra had returned with Cypher to the Drenn watchtower to prepare and wait for the reinforcements to arrive.

They'd found their friends, Captain Salban and Doman, waiting for them there.

"Captain!" Kyro said, when he opened the watchtower door to find her and Doman seated at his kitchen table.

The woman smiled warmly at him. "And so our travelers

have returned. We've been holding down the watchtower for you, and keeping an eye on the skies."

"Th-thank you," Kyro managed to say. "But I thought you hated Star Shepherds."

Salban shrugged. "True, but I don't blame the stars for that."

"I'm so glad you're safe," Doman said, rising to his feet. "I followed you to Romvi, but after that, I couldn't figure out where you'd gone. I was worried. Did you find your father?"

Kyro stared at his shoes, and Andra put a hand on his shoulder. "Sort of," he said.

"What do you mean?" Salban frowned.

Kyro sank into a nearby chair, and Cypher pawed at his knees until he scooped the dog into his lap. "I found my father, but he isn't right. He's not really there. Like he's in some sort of trance." He sighed. "Something happened to him in the Radamak Mountains, but we have no idea how to fix it. I've lost him all over again."

"We'll figure something out, Kyro. I'm sure of it," Andra said, scratching Cypher's ears.

"That's terrible," Salban said. "Perhaps the village doctor can examine him and shed some light on his condition." She glanced around. "Where's your father?"

"He's on the way…" Kyro said. Salban raised an eyebrow at him. "We found him with…with a group of mechanical giants. They're bringing him back here now, along with reinforcements."

"Mechanical giants? Reinforcements? It sounds like you've got quite the tale to tell, and you do owe me a story. Start talking," Salban said.

Kyro explained how they had discovered the giants and uncovered Pelag's plot to cut down all the stars. How Pelag had narrowed his search to Drenn and would attack the skies here in full force next. It was hard to tell which part shocked Salban and Doman the most. But once they recovered, they agreed to help.

They had the rest of the afternoon to prepare, but wasted no time. The giants who arrived with Tirin also brought as many boulders as they could carry from the Radamak Mountains. Now they dug for more to assemble an arsenal.

There was no shortage of amazement from Captain Salban and Doman regarding the giants. Kyro didn't blame them. If he hadn't seen them with his own eyes in the mountains, he wasn't sure he would have believed they were real either.

The giants were quiet and solemn as they worked, silent mechanical sentinels. They harbored no great love for those who had turned against the stars; nevertheless, they didn't relish the prospect of battling their own brethren. But they were crafted with one mission in mind—to protect the stars—and they would do so without hesitation.

While the giants worked, Kyro and Andra did what they could to prepare as well. Captain Salban and Doman headed for the village to collect as many star casings as possible before the sun set. And to warn the villagers that a battle was coming. Kyro knew they'd have to use the catapult mainly against the rogue giants, but they also needed to return as many stars to the sky as possible as they were cut down.

He suspected there would be a lot.

Kyro and Andra set up a makeshift workstation beside their catapult, dragging the table and all the star casings and tools they needed outside. The faster they could use the catapult, the better. Once they were set up, Kyro rummaged through his rucksack for something to eat and found something else instead: that lantern he'd discovered in Sear's star casings. The one Sear had seemed none too pleased he'd taken. He held up to the light to examine it better. It had been an impulsive action, and he wasn't even sure why he'd done it. He'd just known, somehow, the second he'd laid eyes on it that it was important. The lantern was made of a thin, light metal that must have once been bright and shiny, but had begun to dull with age. The inside, however, glowed softly. But it was sealed shut too tightly for Kyro to open.

"What is that?" Andra asked, running a finger over the edge of the lantern.

"I'm not quite sure. I found it with the casings Sear had been hoarding. He didn't seem very happy that I took it."

Andra raised an eyebrow. "Then it must be special. Have you ever seen anything like this with a star before?"

Kyro shook his head, then his breath caught in his throat. Could it be...? "I wonder if this has anything to do with the legends of the Seven Elders or the Elders' Heirs..." He peeked through the decorative swirls cut out on the sides, but all he could see was the soft glowing light, not what was making it.

"I think we should be very careful to keep this safe," Andra said, glancing over her shoulder.

"Agreed." Kyro gently put the lantern back in his pack. Maybe there was some way it could help them turn the tide in this battle. He just had to figure out how.

It was midafternoon before the first of the Flyers arrived, carrying Star Shepherds and their catapults. They first caught a glimpse of them as tiny specks on the horizon, unexpected shapes in the sky. The first Flyer—Elktor—set his shell-shocked burden down near Kyro and his catapult and then took off again immediately.

There were many more Star Shepherds to retrieve before nightfall.

"I'm Kyro," he said, shaking the man's hand. He was a little younger than Tirin and wore a red cloak that clashed with his bright-orange hair.

"Rishi," he said, looking rather green around the gills. "Sorry, today has been a bit of shock. First the giants exist, then the stars are being cut down, and then I have to fly all the way here. Not a thing I ever expected to be doing." To Kyro's surprise, the man laughed. "But certainly a story for the books. I'm happy to help. What's the plan?"

A thrill ran through Kyro's bones, and he and Andra exchanged a knowing smile. This was the first time Kyro was being treated like a real Star Shepherd, instead of a boy who was in the way. His father may not ever know it, but Kyro would try to make him proud.

"We need to set up the catapults strategically around Drenn. Pelag, one of the Elders' heirs, has determined that the star that bears his heart and keeps him alive hangs somewhere overhead. He will try to cut them all down to ensure he can leave this world. We have to save as many stars as possible as quickly as we can."

"And it wouldn't hurt if we can shoot some of those rogue Flyers out of the sky before they can do much damage either," Andra added.

Rishi nodded. "Excellent. Do you have a map of the area?"

Kyro motioned to his workstation. "Here." Rishi examined it, hemmed and hawed and scratched his chin, then straightened up, satisfied.

"Do we know how many more Shepherds are on their way?"

Kyro shook his head. "Not yet. All of them, we hope."

"They'd better. If they don't, they may not be Star Shepherds anymore once this is over." Rishi's eyes flashed, and Kyro decided he liked this man very much. "I'll take my catapult to the edge of the forest on the east to get good coverage here." He picked up a few pebbles from the ground and placed them on the map. "The next few who arrive should go to these marks to cover the whole village. The rest can fill in the spaces in between as needed."

Rishi eyed Kyro's worktable. "Are there more of those casings? They are finely made."

"There will be. The man who crafts them is bringing more back soon. But we should all set up our areas with boulders"—Kyro pointed to the pile of rocks accumulating in the yard—"and star casings to be prepared when the battle begins."

"Understood. Good luck, Kyro." And with that, Rishi rolled his catapult—a wooden version that was much lighter than the one Tirin had crafted—toward the eastern side of the forest.

The rest of the afternoon went on in much the same fashion. Star Shepherds arrived, Kyro and Andra directed them where to go, and all set about their tasks with grim determination. For if they failed, the world would be overrun with darkness. All because of the desire of one ancient man.

Not long before dusk, the last of the Flyers and Star Shepherds arrived. A flurry of activity filled the woods and fields surrounding Kyro's watchtower as everyone finalized their preparations. Captain Salban and Doman returned on their last trip of ferrying star casings.

"Well, Kyro, Andra," Salban said with her hands on her hips, "it looks like you've got yourself quite a fine army." She shook her head as one of the giants lumbered by. "I can't believe you two actually found the giants. To think, they're alive after all this time! It's extraordinary."

Doman marveled at the giants too. "That is some of the finest craftsmanship I've ever seen. Though they could use a good oiling and polishing."

Salban mused, "I wonder if one of them might want to work on my ship. They'd sure come in handy."

Kyro and Andra laughed, the tension hanging over them breaking momentarily.

"You can always ask. But wait until after we've saved the stars, if you please," Kyro said.

The captain chuckled. "Don't worry. I won't be poaching your best soldiers just yet." She tapped Doman on the shoulder. "Let's make sure every catapult has enough boulders to launch."

They set off, and Kyro watched them go. He couldn't help wondering what his father would make of all this if he were himself. As it was, Tirin had spent most of the day inside sleeping, and only an hour or so ago had wandered out of the watchtower and settled in to stare into space and rock back and forth underneath a tree. Though Kyro had tried to talk to him again, his father gave no indication that he was remotely aware of the flurry of activity unfolding before him. A hollow ache filled

Kyro. He'd begun this journey for his father, but it had become so much more. Still, it felt wrong and cruel to have him so close and so far at the same time.

"Kyro!" Andra cried as Cypher began to growl.

The sun had set, and the skies revealed they were no longer alone. The sleek forms of Sear's Flyers soared above them, headed straight for the stars over their heads.

"It's time," Kyro shouted. The nearest Shepherd heard him and took up the cry too. It spread like wildfire across field and forest and village. Boulders wheeled through the night air. Flyers began to drop like stones, but several managed to slice down some of the stars. Shepherds raced to rescue them, sending them right back where they belonged. To Kyro's surprise, Captain Salban was right among them, working a catapult like she'd been doing it all her life.

Kyro sent his boulders at the Flyers, carefully keeping watch for any stars falling near them. Soon, more Flyers had been felled than flew, and against his better judgment, hope began to bloom in Kyro's heart. Maybe this would work after all. Maybe they stood a real chance.

Cypher yapped, circling the catapult, as a star fell near them. Andra rushed to grab it. Together they placed it in its new case and speedily launched it back into the sky. Then a new sound rang out on the battlefield, leaving Kyro chilled. The sound of metal clanging in a steady rhythm. Like hundreds of giants marching upon Drenn. Before he could warn the others, the first of the ground-bound giants loyal to Sear and Pelag broke through the edge of the woods. The stardust didn't hold them back like it had the vissla. They trod over it like useless dirt.

Within minutes, Orers and Crafters swarmed the nearest catapult and began ripping it apart as though it were a child's toy.

CHAPTER THIRTY-ONE

"PROTECT YOUR CATAPULTS!" KYRO AND ANDRA screamed, but it was already too late for the ones on the edge of the forest. The Star Shepherds who manned them fought valiantly against the wave of giants, but were grossly outnumbered. Jector's group ceased loading the catapults with boulders and launched themselves at this new wave of attack.

Captain Salban appeared in front of Kyro and Andra. "We're outnumbered. We'll never win if we don't get more reinforcements. I have an idea." She put a hand on each of their shoulders. "Whatever you do, don't get caught and keep those stars headed skyward."

"Thank you," Kyro said as the captain headed off with a curt nod.

Kyro's stomach turned as he watched giant meet giant in battle. A thousand years ago, they all would have been on the same side, fighting back the dark creatures like the vissla to hang the stars and weave the starlight net. Now, one man's insane plan had divided them. Jector's giants were no match for the larger Orers and Crafters, but they slowed their progress, and that was something. Kyro feared it wouldn't be enough.

The wooden catapults suffered the most, while others like Kyro's were sturdier. Sear's ground army soon learned the difference and targeted the vulnerable catapults, tossing Star Shepherds out of their way like rag dolls. In the sky above, the Flyers loyal to Sear began to slice down the stars with renewed determination.

And all around them stars fell and fell and fell, setting the sky aglow.

Kyro and Andra did their best to retrieve as many as possible. But it was so little in the face of so much destruction. Kyro gritted his teeth. How could this be happening? There had to be some way to stop the rogue giants before the damage was irreversible. If only Tirin was himself, Kyro was sure his father would have some ideas. But the vissla had done something to him.

The spark of an idea began to form in Kyro's mind...

Andra grabbed his arm. "Look!" She pointed at the path to the village and Kyro gaped. He had expected the villagers to run far away or hide in their cellars until the battle was over, but he'd never expected this.

The villagers swarmed the path, breaking through the trees and attacking the rogue giants with all sorts of utensils, from pitchforks to fire pokers to brooms and even a kettle. At the lead were Captain Salban, Doman, and most surprising of all, Bodin.

"It's about time he stopped sulking about everything and did something," Andra said.

"The captain is very convincing," Kyro said, though he was stunned she'd managed to convince the villagers to help. He never would have been able to do that on his own.

"Let's get the rest of these stars, Starboy," Andra said, a smile returning to her face.

Bolstered by the reinforcements, Kyro and Andra completed their work even faster than before. But the stars still rained down, many in their brand-new casings. The catapults that remained, surrounded by an odd mix of giants and villagers, shot down as many rogue Flyers as they could. The giants made horrible crunching sounds as they crashed to the ground. As Kyro and Andra raced to save the stars, they now had to be careful to dodge falling giants too.

Exhaustion began to settle in Kyro's limbs from all the

running, but he didn't dare to stop. Just as he sent the latest star soaring back onto the night's canvas, he noticed his father was no longer sitting beneath the tree. Kyro whirled around, frantically taking in the forest and field that had been transformed into a battleground.

There was his father wandering between huge giants and catapults. And directly into the path of a falling giant. Kyro's stomach dropped into his shoes.

"No!" he cried, startling Andra. Kyro ran headlong toward his father, careening into him moments before the giant smashed into the ground, sending dirt and grass shooting upward. The giant moaned behind them, but his father merely seemed dazed. "The stars..." he murmured.

With shaking limbs, Kyro led his father hurriedly back to the tree where he had been before, a small flicker of hope kindling in his heart.

CHAPTER THIRTY-TWO

IT WAS A LONG SHOT, BUT KYRO HAD TO TRY SOMETHING.
Even something as desperate as this. He pulled his last vial of
stardust from his pack just as Andra appeared at his elbow,
eyeing Tirin with concern. "Is he all right?" she asked. Kyro
shook his head.

"Hard to tell. He seems a bit dazed, but he did say something about the stars. Though who knows if that's because of
the battle or just his old obsession."

"Don't worry. We can keep an eye on him *and* the stars if
we need to."

"I have an idea." Kyro held up the stardust. "It kept the

vissla away before. If my father is like this because of the vissla, maybe this will help him too."

Andra gave the vial a thoughtful look. "It's worth a try." She glanced over her shoulder. "But hurry. We need to get back out there quickly."

Kyro sprinkled some of the dust over his father's head, hoping for the glint of recognition to appear in his eyes. Instead, Tirin's eyes closed, and he slumped back against the tree. It startled Kyro at first, but his father still breathed and appeared otherwise fine. Disappointment filled him. This was not the reaction he'd been hoping for.

"Come on, Starboy," Andra said. "Let him rest. Maybe it just needs a little time to work."

They hurried back into the fray. Flyers dodged and weaved through the boulders rocketing toward them, and the stars still plummeted to the earth. The ground troops and villagers continued to struggle, metal arms clashing against metal swords, wooden staves, and all sorts of mundane items they'd taken up as weapons. There was so much confusion that it became hard to decide who was winning. The best that Kyro and Andra could do from where they stood was dash after the two nearest stars.

Kyro scooped up his star without slowing and returned to the catapult first, deftly slicing the burlap and settling the star into its new casing. A process he and his father had once done reverently was now completed with urgency. As he sent the star back into the sky, he didn't bother to wait to see if it caught. Andra had arrived with hers, and as she sent it back, Kyro waited for another star to fall nearby.

But instead he saw something else. Jector and Sear, clashing fiercely not far away. Sear was huge compared to Jector—which was saying a lot—but Kyro and Andra didn't even stop to think. They each grabbed as many rocks as they could carry and ran toward them.

The sound of the giants' fight was like terrible bells warning of bad news. Before Kyro and Andra could get within throwing distance, Sear stabbed Jector in the torso, sending their friend toppling to the ground. Sear raised his weapon—a rusted sword that looked like it had been made out of discarded parts—over his head, ready to finish off the giant who had risked so much to help them.

Fear spurred Kyro onward, and Andra was right behind.

"Leave him alone," Andra yelled as she hurled a rock and caught Sear on the temple.

Sear roared at them. Kyro threw his rocks too, but the giant, despite his size, was too quick for him. Kyro only grazed Sear's arm. Andra, however, had true aim. Her second rock smashed Sear right in the eye, rendering it useless.

Sear howled, the sound reverberating across the field and rattling Kyro's teeth. Then the giant finally turned his attention to the pair, leaving Jector groaning and forgotten on the ground.

"Foolish children," Sear growled, stomping closer. "You stand no chance of winning."

Kyro pelted the giant's chest with the rest of his rocks, one after the other, but he barely seemed to notice. Andra caught him again on the chin, but Sear shook that off too.

He took two more steps, then halted. His remaining eye, once lit with the magic fires that gave life to all the giants, went black as night. He threw his head back, raising his giant mechanical arms, and screamed.

A familiar, horrible scream that skittered down Kyro's spine like ice.

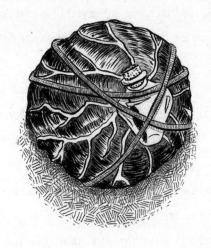

CHAPTER THIRTY-THREE

SHOCK RADIATED THROUGH KYRO, ROOTING HIM TO the ground. Sear was possessed by a vissla! It made an awful sort of sense. No wonder he had been willing to betray his primary function, his reason for existing. It also finally explained why the giants would bother to cut down the stars instead of just stealing them off their hooks; the vissla in them couldn't touch the stars until they were on the ground, free of the Elders' magic. The giants' metal bodies must have offered the vissla some measure of protection from the light of the stars too. The sliced hooks were probably just a product of them being in too great a hurry to be precise when cutting them down. Kyro shuddered as Sear's black eye surveyed him and Andra and the familiar crackling ice began to spread across the field and under their feet.

Without warning, Sear lunged toward Andra, shaking Kyro out of his shock. Before Sear could reach her, Kyro shoved her out of the way. He didn't stop to consider the consequences. He simply acted.

He'd gotten Andra into this mess. She was his only friend. He couldn't bear to see her hurt.

The giant didn't have time to adjust his aim. He loomed over Kyro, his huge metal fist outstretched. It smashed into Kyro's chest, crushing him into the ground.

Pain, hot and bright, stole his breath. Stole his words. A shooting ache spread through his limbs, circling back over and over. Kyro couldn't bring himself to move. Above him, all he could see were the stars. Some glimmering brightly, but so many others were falling to the earth, never to rise again. He heard Andra cry out and felt the nudge of Cypher's cold nose against his cheek. Overwhelming grief rattled through his body.

Then he heard something else. His father's voice. Screaming a single word.

"Kyro!"

Above him, Sear raised his weapon, just as he had over Jector minutes earlier. Kyro wanted so badly to move, but he couldn't do much more than wiggle his arm. Out of the corner of his eye, something glowed.

A new voice cut through the haze surrounding Kyro.

"Stop!" Pelag shouted. "This is not right. This is not what I wanted. I never intended for it to go this far."

Sear cackled, but let his weapon drop to his side. It wasn't the laugh Kyro had heard from the others. It was tainted with the cold crackling screech of the vissla that possessed the giant. Sear bent toward him and Kyro cringed, fearing he meant to finish him off. But instead, Sear plucked something from the ground near Kyro. The object that had been glowing out of the corner of his eye. When the giant lifted it up, Kyro realized it was the lantern that he had tucked into his pack. It must have fallen out when Sear punched him. Regret burst over him. He'd hoped he could find a way to use that in the battle, but now it was too late.

Another wave of pain flooded Kyro, but he tried to focus on what was happening around him instead. The giant opened the lantern easily and tipped it over into his metal palm. The still-glowing heart of a star clinked in his hand. This one looked like a perfect, clear crystal, cut like an octagonal diamond. But something else was attached to the star. A small glass vial with something inside it, red and crystalline. Kyro's breathing was already ragged, and now it nearly stopped. He had a sneaking suspicion he knew exactly what the something was.

A heart of an Elder or their heirs, given to the stars long, long ago, and somehow kept alive by that lantern.

Sear raised the heart and vial over his head, and smashed them to the ground. Light burst from the star as it shattered, blinding them all. Pelag moaned and staggered, then fell to his knees clutching his chest.

The heart Sear had been hoarding was Pelag's. He must have hidden it when he found it so that the vissla possessing him could have an excuse to continue destroying stars.

Kyro's back began to grow cold. At first, it occurred to him that it was because of his injury and that there may not be any coming back from it. But then he heard it: the crackling of ice and the slick feel of it sliding across the ground, freezing his shoulders and feet. Shrieks began to echo from all sides. The cold wormed all the way into Kyro's bones, making him completely numb.

Vissla. Many, many vissla.

CHAPTER THIRTY-FOUR

THE SHADOWS IN THE FOREST CAME ALIVE, SEEPING out from between the trees to surround Kyro and his friends. The cold and ice crawled over everything near them—Kyro's catapult, his worktable, the star casings, even Cypher's tail that had ceased its wagging the moment Kyro was injured.

Sadness fell over Kyro. Pelag lay not far from him, the life slowly slipping out of them both, helpless to do anything to stop the madness Sear wished to unleash. The possessed giant had begun to rant again, and Kyro couldn't help but hear, though he was having a hard time keeping his eyes open for more than a minute or two now.

Sear towered over Pelag's body, sneering at the ancient man. "I found your heart weeks ago, old man. But I hid it. You inspired the others to continue cutting down the stars. It was useful to keep you around for a bit longer. Luckily, we still had a few of the old lanterns the Elders used to contain the light that held the darkness at bay before they devised the plan to craft stars and form the starlight net. Now, we shall cut *all* the stars down!" Sear threw his long metal arms into the air and cackled. "And with you gone, Pelag, there will be no one left to bear the secrets of crafting stars. The world will at last return to its true, rightful form—a world ruled by night, and the vissla and our kin."

Pelag coughed and wheezed, but managed to squeak out. "Sear, you have lost your way. You were good and loyal for many centuries." He coughed again. "It is the vissla inside you. I know the giant you truly are is in there somewhere. Fight it, Sear, or all hope is lost!"

Sear threw his head back and laughed with a clashing roar. "Fool. The vissla and I are one. And of one mind. You shall die, and we shall rule."

Kyro could hardly focus anymore. The crash of the battle that continued to rage around them had faded to a dull roar. Above him, the faces of Andra and his father whispered and leaked teardrops as their hands stroked his hair and face.

"Kyro," whispered his father. "I'm so sorry I disappeared

on you. I thought I could stop the stars from being taken on my own, but I was wrong. I shouldn't have left you. You've been a better partner than I've ever given you credit for. Just hang on, son. Please. Then we can watch the stars together. I promise."

Kyro closed his eyes. He'd waited so long to hear words like those. Waited so long to have his father back. He tried to say something comforting, but all that came out was a groan.

Andra gripped his hand. "Don't you dare give up, Starboy."

Kyro would miss them both. He didn't want to leave them now, not really. He wanted to stay. But the pull was magnetic. Irresistible.

From the corner of his eye, he spied Pelag motioning to him. Kyro blinked, not sure what the old man wanted. His brain seemed to be thinking through a thick fog, slow and ambling and in no hurry.

Suddenly Kyro realized that Pelag was gesturing to something that rested against Kyro's outstretched arm. It remained where it had fallen after Sear's blow, and Kyro hadn't yet had the will or desire to try to move his arm much. Moving hurt. But Pelag seemed to think the thing was important. Kyro could see in the old man's eyes that the pull to the other side was dragging him away too, but he resisted just to communicate this to Kyro.

Kyro wrapped his fingers around the object and managed to pull it close enough to examine it. Warm shock melted some

of the ice inside him as he realized it was a shard from the star's heart, still aglow with life and light. Pelag motioned to his chest, miming an action, and with a sudden rush Kyro understood.

He knew what he needed to do.

Kyro moved his hand over his heart, positioning the shard just above it. His breath was shallow and gasping as it was, and he didn't dare to examine the cause. He glanced over at Pelag again; the old man smiled and nodded and mimed the action one more time. Kyro wasn't sure what the shard could do exactly, but Pelag seemed certain this would help.

Kyro rested his hands on top of the shard and shoved the piece of star into his chest as hard as he could. Andra, who had been watching this silent exchange, understood without him having to ask. She placed her own hands on top of Kyro's and pushed the shard the rest of the way into his chest.

CHAPTER THIRTY-FIVE

AMID THE SEARING PAIN, KYRO COULD HEAR THE VISSLA screaming. He vaguely saw the shadow of the possessed giant lunge for him, though there was nothing he could do to stop him. But Sear never reached Kyro. Something else—Jector, Kyro suspected—pounced on the opportunity and sliced Sear's head from his body. The horrible scream of metal on metal rivaled the vissla cries. Then the giant's head rolled over the ground, settling near where Kyro lay. Sear's black-glowing eyes flickered out into a dull, dead gray.

Pain surged through his body anew, but Kyro could make no sound. He didn't have the strength anymore. But he knew his father was there, and so was Andra. They held on to him, keeping him from slipping away as the shard from the star's heart melted into him, becoming one with his human form.

Suddenly, warmth flooded his veins. Brilliant light flared, pouring from his eyes and mouth. Everything was bright as day despite the late hour. The screams of the vissla reached a fever pitch as they shrank back from the light. To Kyro, everything else had gone still. There was only the warmth, the light, and the feeling of those two things coursing through his broken body. Changing it. Renewing it. Healing it.

Kyro's back arched as a new burst of light exploded from his chest, bathing the battleground in pure, white light. He couldn't see the extent of it, but it at least reached all the way into the trees and as far as the village. Later, there would be those who'd say it could even be seen from the harbor.

The vissla went silent.

The light faded, and Kyro sat up, released from whatever hold it had on him. He touched his chest gingerly, marveling at the new skin that had healed over the wound. Cypher leapt into his lap, immediately covering his face in kisses. Tirin wrapped his arms around his son, pulling him close.

"Thank the stars you're all right, Kyro," he said. "I don't know what I'd do if I lost you."

Kyro hugged his father back. Perhaps this time things really would be different. And he might not feel so forgotten anymore.

"I knew you'd make it, Starboy." Andra grinned, though Kyro suspected that was a tear or two he spied shimmering in the corner of her eyes.

He glanced around. "The vissla. They're all gone."

Andra nodded. "They were no match for you."

Pelag moaned nearby. "Kyro," he whispered through a smile. "I'll be gone soon. At last." The ancient man fumbled to reach into his pocket, then stretched his arm out over the ground toward Kyro. "Take this."

Kyro disentangled himself from his friends and knelt near the dying man. Pelag took his hand and pressed something cool and metal into it. "Keep this close, always. Someone must protect the secrets of the stars. I have carried that burden much too long. Now it is up to you. With this"—Pelag gestured to the object in Kyro's hand—"and that"—he pointed to Kyro's chest—"you will have everything you need to learn those secrets and keep them safe. I was wrong, Kyro. Very wrong. I should have listened when you came to me. The evil remains, and the stars are needed to keep the world safe. Maybe more than that. Take this task seriously. You must not forget, not like I did. Promise me."

Kyro opened his hand to find a very old, ornate key lying in his palm. "I promise."

"Then I can finally be at peace." Pelag's chest rose and fell one last time, then the light faded from his eyes. He was still.

Tirin put his hand on Kyro's shoulder. "From now on, we'll protect the stars together, son. That's a promise."

That was all Kyro had ever wanted. To feel like a part of his own family again.

CHAPTER THIRTY-SIX

WITH SEAR FELLED, PELAG DEAD, AND THE VISSLA BAN-
ished, the giants ceased fighting the Star Shepherds. Many of
them appeared dazed, which made Kyro wonder how many
others aside from Sear had been possessed by one of the dark
creatures. Whatever the cause, whether for Pelag's desperation
or Sear's dark aims, their reason for fighting was gone. Many
of the Flyers simply zoomed off into the night, headed in the
direction of their camp in the Radamak Mountains. Others like
the Crafters and Orers remained behind to help clean up the
destruction wrought by the battle.

Soon Star Shepherds and giants worked side by side,

picking up the pieces of broken catapults and mechanical giants, and fixing what they could. Captain Salban, Doman, and the rest of the villagers joined in too, much to Kyro's surprise and gratitude. Without all this help, it would've taken days to clean up.

Jector stooped next to Kyro. Tirin regarded him almost as though he was seeing the giant for the first time, despite having spent several days living with him.

"I am glad to see you have found yourself, Tirin," Jector said. "It is good to meet you again."

Tirin nodded. "I am not entirely sure what happened to me or how I came out of it, but I suspect I am greatly indebted to you and your friends."

"Something shocked you into a trance in the Radamak Mountains," Kyro said. "Jector and his friends took you in. Apparently, you were very good at fixing them, despite the trance."

Tirin laughed. "That wasn't a dream then? I do remember something sort of like that. How very strange and wonderful. Though I am glad to be back to normal now."

Kyro scuffed his shoe on the grass. "About that. I tried sprinkling stardust on you in the hopes it would undo whatever the vissla did to you. It didn't seem to work at first, but perhaps it took a little time to sink in."

His father smiled and put his arm around Kyro's shoulders.

"Perhaps it did. I've always known stardust had protective qualities. It could be capable of much more than we realize."

Jector scooped up something shimmering on the ground nearby—the shattered remains of the star that had borne Pelag's heart. He handed the pieces to Kyro, who took them reverently.

"This is a very old star. You may wish to keep it. The older the star, the more powerful it is."

"What do you mean?" Kyro asked.

"They—and the one in your chest—will give you some protection. And a better understanding of the stars."

Kyro rubbed his chest. He no longer felt any pain at all, just a pleasant sort of warmth. "Do you know what happened when I put the shard in my chest? Pelag showed me what to do, but he didn't have time to explain."

Jector frowned. "As far as I know, this has never been done before. I believe that, just like the Elders gave their hearts to the stars to protect humankind, this star gave its heart to *you*. It needed to meld with you in order to protect you and banish the vissla. But who knows what else it might do?" The giant shrugged.

"What about the lantern? I carried that for far longer than I've ever seen a star survive without hanging in the sky."

"Yes, that was how the Elders first kept the darkness away. The lanterns are imbued with the Elders' magic so that the light won't fade. There are not many left. You should keep that safe too." Jector rose to his feet. "Good luck, Kyro. And thank you for alerting us to the danger to the stars. I do not care to imagine what might have happened had you not." Jector managed a mechanical shudder, then lumbered off to help the others.

Kyro tucked the broken pieces of the star back into the lantern. It might come in handy later, especially if this would help them retain a little of their magic.

As Jector left Kyro's side, Captain Salban made her way over with a strange expression on her face. She pulled Kyro aside and put her hands on both his shoulders, staring him straight in the eyes. "How are you feeling?"

A wave of uneasiness washed over him at her question. "Fine," he said. "Better than fine, really. I thought I was done for, but that shard of star heart healed me somehow."

Salban stared at him for a moment longer, then released her grip. "Good. I'm glad to hear it. But Pelag has given you a greater responsibility than you may realize. That star gave you its heart."

Kyro frowned. "That's what Jector said."

"Do you recall the stories of how the Elders and their heirs gave a part of their hearts to the stars?"

He nodded.

"Well, perhaps this is something like the reverse." Salban smiled wryly. "Maybe that star will live on in you."

Her words made him all the more curious as to what Jector meant by a better understanding of the stars. A shiver brushed

over Kyro's shoulders, but he chalked it up to the night breeze. "It helped me live, so I'm grateful for it."

"As you should be." The captain's eyes narrowed. "What was it that Pelag gave you before he died?"

Kyro took the key from his pack, and Salban's eyes went wide. "Well, well, well," she murmured. "It seems he's given you all his secrets after all. Keep that safe, and keep it close. Don't tell anyone else you have it. The fewer people who know, the better."

"Why?" Kyro asked.

"Trust me. Promise me you'll keep it secret." Captain Salban's face was unusually grim.

"I promise." Kyro decided to risk pressing the question. "But what does it unlock? You must know if you feel the need to make me promise."

Salban's eyes twinkled as she leaned closer. "Clever boy. It unlocks the secrets of the stars. Someday perhaps I'll tell you a story about it. Until then, guard it well." Kyro's mouth hung open, and she patted him on the shoulder and smiled. "Now go join your father. I'm sure you have a lot of catching up to do."

Kyro did, though he was still curious to learn more about the captain and her connection to the stars. As she resumed helping the cleanup, Andra approached her with sparkling eyes. "Captain, before you and your crew leave, might I see your ship by any chance? Sailing sounds like a wonderful adventure!"

The captain laughed. "It is indeed. Come by the docks tomorrow. I'll give you a tour."

"And perhaps I can hear about some of your own adventures?"

"I suppose it's only fair, since I've heard all about yours."

Andra grinned and continued working beside Captain Salban and occasionally asking her questions.

Kyro and his father worked side by side, retrieving fallen stars and placing them in new cases as quickly as possible. But when Kyro stumbled upon the wreckage of one particular star, his breath caught in his chest. The glass case was shattered, but the star's light still shone bright and silver through the mess. Next to it was a handkerchief, and a little heart and puppy both made of gears.

This was his mother's star. The very first one he and his father had returned to the heavens.

Kyro tugged on his father's sleeve, unable to find the words.

"What is it, son?" Tirin said. Kyro pointed, choking back a sob swelling in his throat.

His father knelt beside the broken casing. "It's hers," he whispered.

Without hesitation, Tirin carefully picked the star and the tokens out of the wreckage and carried them gently to a new case set out nearby. He set them inside and placed his hand on Kyro's shoulder.

"Don't worry, this time we can save her." Together they secured the top of the case over the star and set it with the others ready to return to the sky.

With all the extra help, the job was soon nearly done. Andra and Tirin stood beside Kyro as Flyers began to soar straight up into the sky. So many stars had been cut down, and too many catapults destroyed. Now, the quickest way to keep the stars safe was the original way—by giant, flying straight into the sky and hanging the stars with care in the self-hooking glass and steel cases of the Star Shepherds. Jector personally hung the star with Sanna's tokens—right over the Drenn watchtower so it would sparkle there for long after new owners had moved in.

Kyro took Andra's hand and smiled as they watched the stars in the sky increase, sparkling and twinkling as brightly as ever. And with every star that joined the sky, Kyro felt a slight tug, right where that shard should be, as if it would have liked to join them if it could.

When all the stars were hung, the crowd began to disperse. The villagers went home, and Flyers helped the Star Shepherds return to their many corners of the world. Andra and Tirin helped Kyro back inside the watchtower to rest.

And all the way, Kyro glowed a soft, white light.

EPILOGUE

NIGHT FELL SOFTLY OVER THE VILLAGE OF DRENN, PAINT-
ing the sky with dreamy dark strokes. The stars peeked out,
twinkling high above, as Kyro and Andra walked the now well-
worn path from the village to the Star Shepherd's watchtower.
When they reached the workshop, a man opened the door and
bid Kyro's father good night.

"Good evening, Kyro, Andra," said Shane, the village leader
and tailor. "Just picking up this little contraption here." He held
up a small clockwork machine. "It's supposed to make sewing
easier and faster. I may be able to take on more repairs and
commissions if it works."

"Very nice," Andra said with a knowing look at Kyro. Only a few months ago, Shane had told Tirin and Kyro they were unwelcome in the village. But now, thanks to Tirin's ingenious clockwork inventions, the villagers were warming up to him. After Kyro and his father returned from the Radamak Mountains, Tirin had become a new man. Something had changed in him at last, as if he'd woken up from a long, deep sleep. He converted his workshop into a new clock shop and threw his heart into it. Kyro had taken over the responsibilities for the stars—with the blessing of the Star Shepherd Council, of course. Andra came over to help every chance she got.

They waved to Shane and entered the clock shop, just in time to see Kyro's father closing up. He stopped what he was doing and put his arm around his son's shoulders. "You're just in time, Kyro. It's been a while since I made a real dinner, and I know you need nourishment while you watch those stars. Plus, I wanted to try out this new oven I've been working on. There's a casserole in the kitchen for you two to share."

"Thanks," Kyro said. He still hadn't gotten used to this new side of his father. All he knew was that he wasn't going to take it for granted for a second.

"It smells wonderful," Andra said.

As they neared the kitchen, Cypher bounded over to greet them, tongue lolling and tail wagging happily. Kyro laughed and scratched the dog's ears. Kyro and Andra quickly served themselves steaming casserole in bowls and then hurried up the stairs to the watchtower. Cypher followed them with a yap; he wanted casserole too.

Things had also changed for Kyro. Ever since the battle, he hadn't needed his starglass goggles anymore. He could sense the stars and where they had fallen even before he could see them with his eyes. The star inside him always recognized its brothers and sisters. And sometimes he felt an odd tug inside his chest that threatened to send him wandering over the hills. He hadn't given in to it yet, but he knew one day he would. He had the sneaking suspicion it might lead him to whatever that key was meant to unlock.

Tonight, Kyro and Andra sat in the watchtower chair together, and it slowly made its rounds while they ate their dinner. Just as they set aside their bowls, the darkening sky flashed and a single star fell to the earth. Kyro leaned forward, eager to see where it landed. When he looked back, Andra already had her starglass goggles on and a grin spreading over her face. The Council had made her an honorary Star Shepherd after the battle with the rogue giants, and she had prized her goggles ever since.

"Hurry up, Starboy. Or I'll beat you to it."

Kyro glanced up once more at the stars, letting their glow fill him in a new strange way. Then he and Cypher raced after Andra and the fallen star, heedless of the darkness.

The glow was a part of him now, and it never led him astray.

ACKNOWLEDGMENTS

Dan Haring

This story has been a long time in the making. It began as an animated short film I started making way back in 2007. In 2011, it began its journey to becoming a book, and what you're holding is the culmination of all that time. It would be impossible for me to remember to thank everyone who has helped and supported me and this story through the years, but I am truly grateful to all who have.

To my wife Kori, and our kids: You are the stars in my sky. I'm truly blessed to have your love and support.

To my agent, Kathleen Ortiz, who saw the potential in this story and who has worked tirelessly to help it become a reality. Without you this book would not exist. Thank you for believing in it and me.

To MarcyKate Connolly, who agreed to go on this journey

with me and has been the best collaborator I could have asked for. I will forever be grateful for your love for Kyro and this story and the way you weaved your magic throughout it.

To Suzie Townsend, for being willing to share MarcyKate, as well as Joanna Volpe, Pouya Shahbazian, and the whole team at New Leaf Literary & Media.

To our editor, Annie Berger, as well as Jordan Kost and the entire team at Sourcebooks. Your insight and feedback were invaluable, and you pushed the story to new heights.

Special thanks to Mom and Dad, who have always supported me. Also to Tamlynn, Mikey, and Kristen for making growing up the awesome experience it was, and to their spouses for becoming part of our family. To my wife's family, who have treated me as one of their own from the very first day, and to my cousins for their love and support.

To Goshen, for being a small enough town that my imagination had plenty of room to run wild.

To all the art and English teachers I've ever had, especially Mrs. White, Mrs. Bridges, Mrs. Burdick, and Mr. Bills. Thanks to Brent Adams, Kelly Loosli, Ryan Woodward, and friends from BYU Animation.

To Marni Hoopes and the Hoopes family, who have been supporters of this story since day one.

To the Novel Nineteens group for being such an amazing and supportive group of people. And a special shout-out to the MG authors, who are some of the best people I've ever met.

To D. Michael Hansen, for creating the beautiful music for the short film and being a great friend since junior high. And to Blake Johnson and Jacob Speirs for their help with the short film.

To Jakris Smittant, for letting me use your awesome name.

To my brothers at Strange Reptile, for letting me make cool new worlds every day.

To Blizzard, for being the model for Cypher.

To friends who gave feedback, ideas, and support: Cade and Amy Adams, Mike and Brit Murdock, Glenn and Kristen Harmon, Blake and Natasha Johnson, Brett and KT Shumway, Mike and Vanessa Hansen, Heather Dixon Wallwork, Dustin Hansen, Natalie Lloyd, Jennifer Rush, D.J. Kirkbride, Lea Hernandez Seidman, Phillip Sevy, Dan Naughton, Misty Bott, Mike Zahajko, Moroni Taylor, and the Carter, May, and Tavares families, and the rest of the Danbury tribe, everyone else who has supported me in this endeavor, and anyone I might have forgotten. I wish I could thank you each personally.

Thanks to the Bouncing Souls, Social Distortion, Chuck Ragan, Tiger Army, and the Menzingers, for being the soundtrack while I wrote and drew.

To Batman, because he's awesome.

And finally, thank YOU for picking up this book and taking a chance on it.

The Star Shepherd is a very special book, one I'm so grateful I've had the opportunity to be a part of. From the moment my agent pitched me the project, I've adored this story and these characters. So, first and foremost, thank you to Dan Haring for creating this storyworld and allowing me to be a part of it. And for bringing it to life with all his amazing illustrations too! (I cannot draw to save my life, so they seem like little miracles to me.)

This book wouldn't have happened without our agents, Suzie Townsend and Kathleen Ortiz—thank you so much for your brilliant idea to pair us up for this book. And of course, the rest of the team at New Leaf, particularly Cassandra Baim, Pouya Shahbazian, and Sara Stricker.

So many thanks to the incredible folks at Sourcebooks! Extra special thanks to our fantastic editor, Annie Berger, and her editorial assistant, Sarah Kasman, and the rest of their small army behind the scenes for all their time and effort on this book—we are so lucky to work with you!

As always, thank you to my family for all your love, support, and understanding while I've seemingly been under near constant deadlines this past year. You make everything worth it.

And finally, thank you, readers. I hope you love this story as much as we do!

Read on for a peek into
SHADOW WEAVER,
the first book in MarcyKate Connolly's

magical Shadow Weaver duology

CHAPTER ONE

THE FIRST TIME MY SHADOW SPOKE TO ME, I was a mere infant in the cradle. They say that on the night I was born, even the stars fled the sky and the moon hid under a dark cloak. That I was a quiet thing, with a shock of black hair and eyes like glittering onyx. I did not scream like other newborn children. And I did not reach for my mother like instinct should have instructed me.

Instead, I held out my tiny arms and smiled at the shadow in the corner of the room.

And it smiled back.

It's my favorite sort of day: stormy. Rain pelts the mansion in a wild rhythm, and the shadows shiver between the trees outside my windows. Everything is cast in lovely shades of darkness.

Dar—my shadow—is restless beside me, pacing from one corner of the room to the other. *Kendra is late*, she says. *We should play a game outside instead. Can't you hear the shadows calling to us?*

While the offer is tempting, I want to see Kendra today. At thirteen, she is a year older than me, and her mother is a maid. We play together sometimes, but I've barely seen her since she began working in our mansion a couple of months ago. Mother only allowed me to play with Kendra before she was a servant; now she says it isn't proper to socialize with the help.

Except for Dar, I've never had many friends, and I miss having Kendra around. The Cerelia Comet blessed me with magic, and I was born with the talent of shadow weaving. When I was little, I kept myself entertained by crafting toys from the shadows and playing with the one tethered to my feet. Dar is the only shadow that is my friend. To most people, shadows are things that remain stuck to walls and floors, but for me, they become whatever I wish—tacky, like clay, or as thin as smoke. I can mold them all to my will. Now that I'm older, my shadowcraft has improved. Before me on the low table in the sitting room is an array of shadows I've plucked from the corners of the mansion. A dark teapot steams next to three teacups and saucers. A smoky tray holds real biscuits—shadows don't taste very good—and three carved wooden chairs wait for Kendra to arrive so we can all take our seats.

Mother is not aware that I invited Kendra to tea today. I do have other games I'd rather play with Dar and the shadows, but Kendra doesn't seem to like them much. So tea it is.

Dar settles at my feet for a few moments before we hear a sound in the hallway. Hope warms me, but it is only one of the other servants walking by. I sink into a chair as disappointment swells inside my chest. Kendra is nearly half an hour late. I know she has duties, but she could have come by for a moment or at least sent a note explaining her absence.

Perhaps your mother kept her away, Dar suggests. *She doesn't like to have you playing with the help anymore.*

"You're probably right," I scowl. My mother has no trouble keeping her servants busy. And she does her best to keep everyone away from me.

I sit up straighter. "Let's bring Kendra a gift. It might be fun to sneak down to the servants' quarters after dinner."

Dar curves into a smile on the floor. *Does this mean we can go outside now?*

I laugh despite the strange heaviness weighing on me. The storm has nearly passed, and the sun is disappearing beyond the horizon. Even now, tiny specks of light flicker among the shadows on our lawn.

I pick up a jar from a nearby shelf, and Dar and I hurry outside before Mother can scold me for playing in the damp weather. The darkness deepens around us as we enter the woods by my home, the shadows cast by the trees reaching their limbs toward us in welcome. My feet begin to move, and I weave between the moss-covered trunks while Dar hums a tune. Together we dance in the gloaming, coaxing shadows and fireflies into the jar. By the time the jar is full, I am breathless from laughter, but not enough to forget the hollowness that blossomed when Kendra didn't appear this afternoon.

"Emmeline!" My mother's voice stops my feet in their tracks.

"We better hurry or we'll be late for dinner." I secure the lid on my jar. Dar sighs but follows, her shape angling toward the trees like she'd rather remain outdoors. When I close the door behind me, she is at my side again. Even if Mother does keep me from Kendra, I am never alone. I always have Dar to keep me company.

In the jar, the shadows swirl around tiny flitting dots of light. Kendra always liked pretty things, and these shadows are so lovely, I'm sure she'll like them too. I hope Mother hasn't been working her too hard. I slip the jar into a hidden pocket in my skirts.

"Emmeline!" Mother calls again.

"Coming," I call back, and hasten toward the dining room.

After dinner, Dar and I pretend to head for my rooms; then, when Mother and Father aren't looking, I cloak myself in shadows and we sneak down to the servants' quarters. Kendra and her parents share a room, and I've visited her there once or twice before. She is probably tired from a hard day and forgot all about our tea.

But when Dar and I hover outside her door, ready to knock, I hear voices. My hand pauses inches away from the wooden slats. It is one of the older serving girls, and she and Kendra are laughing. A pang of jealousy shoots through me. Kendra has never laughed with me like that.

"Emmeline invited you to play tea? Even though she's twelve years old?"

I flinch. It isn't my fault we only play tea. Kendra refuses to play any other shadow games.

Kendra groans through the door, and I can picture her tossing her pale hair over her shoulders. "She's crazy. Shadow weavers may be able to make things from shadows—which is bizarre enough—but they're not supposed to be able to hear and talk to them too. None of the comet-blessed have more than one talent—everyone knows that. But she honestly believes her shadow is a living thing. She even talks to it and pretends it talks back. She's insane!"

Heat flashes over my entire body. I brace myself with one hand against the door frame. Their tinkling laughter feels like glass striking my eardrums. Dar growls.

I may be the only one who can hear Dar, but that doesn't mean I'm mad.

She isn't worth our time, Emmeline. She has a cruel heart. All those times she played and made nice when she really thinks you're crazy! Dar huffs. To them she is only a shadow stuck to the floors and walls, but to me she is so much more. *We're better off without her.*

The other serving girl finds her voice again. "Well, it's a good thing you didn't go. You know what they say about what happened to that neighbor girl, Rose."

Kendra's laughter tapers off. "Emmeline is just crazy enough to be dangerous."

My heart sinks all the way into the ground. I shift the jar of shadows in my hands, my palms suddenly slick, and the fireflies wink. The way the dark and light play off each other is beautiful, but I realize now that Kendra never would have appreciated this gift.

She didn't say a word hinting at her true feelings when the three of us played with my shadow dolls and drank tea from teapots made of smoke. It was a game she only pretended to enjoy.

She was never my friend at all.

"You're right, Dar." I climb back up the stairs to my rooms, and the heat begins to vanish, until all I can feel is cold.

Later that night, while Dar comforts me in my quarters, running her cool fingers through my hair and brushing the tears from my cheeks, the fireflies' lights go out. I curl into a ball on my bed and send the swirling shadows back to the woods, with a promise that from now on, I'll only share them with those who will truly appreciate them.

ABOUT THE AUTHORS

Dan Haring is a visual effects and animation artist who has worked on films such as *Tangled*, *The Lion King 3-D*, *The Incredible Hulk*, and *Rio 2*. He is currently helping create new worlds in virtual reality at Strange Reptile. He loves comic books, especially Batman. He lives in Utah with his awesome wife and kids.

MarcyKate Connolly is a *New York Times* bestselling children's book author who lives in New England with her family and a grumble of pugs. She graduated from Hampshire College (a magical place where they don't give you grades) where she wrote an opera sequel to *Hamlet* as the equivalent of senior thesis. It was also there that she first fell in love with plotting and has been dreaming up new ways to make life difficult for her characters ever since. You can visit her online at marcykate.com.